IGGY LOOMIS
SUPERKID IN TRAINING

JENNIFER ALLISON
··· *Illustrated by* **MIKE MORAN** ···

DIAL BOOKS FOR YOUNG READERS *An imprint of Penguin Group (USA) Inc.*

DIAL BOOKS FOR YOUNG READERS
A division of Penguin Young Readers Group • *Published by the Penguin Group*
Penguin Group (USA) Inc., 375 Hudson Street, New York, New York 10014, USA

USA | Canada | UK | Australia | New Zealand | Ireland | India | South Africa | China
Penguin Books Ltd, Registered Offices: 80 Strand, London WC2R 0RL, England • For more
information about the Penguin Group visit penguin.com

LIBRARY OF CONGRESS CATALOGING-IN-PUBLICATION DATA
Allison, Jennifer.
Superkid in training / by Jennifer Allison. ; illustrated by Michael Moran.
p. cm. — (Iggy Loomis ; bk. 1)
Summary: Just as Daniel is adjusting to sharing his room with Iggy, his little brother, a strange
boy with a big interest in bugs moves into their neighborhood, providing Daniel with a new
friend but Iggy with some mutated DNA. • ISBN 978-0-8037-3759-4 (hardcover)
[1. Brothers—Fiction. 2. Family life—Fiction. 3. Extraterrestrial beings—Fiction.
4. Mutation (Biology)—Fiction. 5. Science fiction.] I. Title.
PZ7.A4428Sup 2013   [Fic]—dc23
2012017462

Printed in USA • 10 9 8 7 6 5 4 3 2 1
Designed by Jason Henry • Text set in Napoleone Slab
The publisher does not have any control over and does not assume any
responsibility for author or third-party websites or their content.

To my favorite young readers:
Max, Marcus, and Gigi!
–J.A.

To my superkids, Patrick and Matthew
–M.M.

ACKNOWLEDGMENTS

Thank you to Doug Stewart, Maureen Sullivan, and Lauri Hornik, who first encouraged me to write this book, and to Andrew Harwell, who oversaw several drafts of the manuscript. A very special thank-you to my editor Lucia Monfried for her insight, patience, and excellent editorial guidance. Mike Moran: thanks for collaborating and for bringing Iggy's world to life with your fantastic art. Rosanne Lauer and Stacey Friedberg: thank you for your attention to so many details. Jason Henry: thank you for your excellent book design. Finally, I want to thank young reader Henry Rosser, who wanted Iggy to have "more cool powers," and my son Max, who was the very first reader for *Iggy Loomis*.

·1·

DANIEL LOOMIS AND THE LITTLE BROTHER INVASION

I KNEW IT WOULD HAPPEN eventually, but I didn't think my nightmare would come true quite so *soon*. Well, it happened today: My parents decided to move my little brother, Iggy, into my bedroom.

Big deal, Daniel, you're probably thinking. Lots of kids have to share bedrooms with their brothers and sisters and they don't whine about it. A few of them even like it.

Did I mention that Iggy has only been potty trained for a few months?

And in case you're picturing a cute little toddler, did I mention that Iggy breaks almost everything he touches? For example, if you have any breakable Planet Blaster Technoblok spacecraft models that you've just spent five hours building and Iggy walks into the room, you'd better plan on redoing all your work because Iggy can break an entire squadron of spaceships in about one second.

And if you don't like loud noises, you'd better buy some earplugs in case you happen to be within fifty feet of Iggy when he gets frustrated about something, which is about half of the time he's awake.

So why is Iggy moving into my room now instead of sharing a room with his twin sister, Dottie?

Because Iggy destroyed his crib, and now he needs a new bed. My parents figure my bunk bed would be the perfect spot for him. Anyway, it all started this morning when Iggy and Dottie were bouncing on their crib mattresses and yelling, "Oh, yeah! Oh, yeah!!"

Suddenly, I heard a loud *CRASH!*, and then a more quiet, "Uh-oh."

Dottie piped up: "Iggy bwoke his bed!"

My parents and I hurried into Iggy and Dottie's room and stared at Iggy's crib. It had totally collapsed; Iggy's mattress was on the floor.

"That's it," said Mom. "The crib won't hold him anymore; he needs a bigger bed."

"He needs a bigger *home*," said Dad. Dad likes to joke about sending all three of his kids to live on a farm somewhere. I know he's kidding, sort of.

"Maybe we could get him a big cage," I suggested, "like the monkey house at the zoo."

"My bed bwoke!" Iggy announced. As if we still needed to have that part explained.

"I think it's time," said Mom.

"Time for the monkey cage?" I asked.

"Time for Iggy's move-in day."

I knew what was coming next. "Oh, no," I said. "No way!"

"Daniel, you knew that you and Iggy would need to share a room. You two boys together. This is just a bit sooner than we expected."

"Your mother's right," said my dad. "Iggy needs a new bed, and you've got a bunk bed."

"He can sleep on your bottom bunk, and you can have the top," Mom added.

"But it actually makes more sense for Iggy

and Dottie to share a room," I protested, "because they LIKE each other."

It's true that Iggy and Dottie usually get along amazingly well. Maybe it's because they're twins. Maybe it's because Dottie doesn't own any toy spaceships or robots that Iggy can break. Maybe it's because Iggy actually enjoys dressing up in Dottie's princess costumes and playing her twirlie-twirl game, which usually ends with them crashing into something and breaking it.

"Iggy could move in with you and Dad," I suggested.

"He can't share a room with us," said Mom.

"Why not?"

"Because he can't."

My parents obviously didn't want to share a room with Iggy any more than I did.

"Iggy, honey, let's get your things ready to move to Daniel's room," said Mom.

"Daniel's room? Oh YAY! AWESOME!" Iggy was thrilled. "Daniel's room! COOL!"

"HE'S NOT MOVING TO MY ROOM!" I shouted. Then I went to my room to think. I considered my options:

1. I could barricade the door to my room. (No, not realistic; Mom and Dad would get in somehow.)

2. I could move down to the basement. (No—too many spiders down there.)

3. I could roll Iggy in a sleeping bag and throw him out the window. (Too difficult. Iggy would fight like a wild animal if I tried to trap him in a blanket.)

It had finally happened. I was cornered with no escape from the little brother invasion. I looked at my favorite Planet Blaster models and sighed. I knew what would happen: Iggy would want to play with all my toys, and within hours, he would break everything.

· 2 ·

SELF-DEFENSE

WHILE IGGY GOT READY to move into my room, I decided to get ready for the Little Brother Invasion.

I have to defend myself and my way of life, I thought. It was a matter of survival.

I moved my favorite Planet Blaster models up to the top bunk so I could guard them more easily. It was going to be very uncomfortable trying to sleep with all that hard plastic around me, but at least everything would be far away from Iggy.

I heard my mom, dad, and Iggy packing up Iggy's clothes and comforting Dottie as Iggy got ready to move out of the bedroom they had shared ever since they were newborn babies. "I come back, Dottie," said Iggy. "I visit you next day."

Within a couple of seconds, Iggy appeared in my doorway, waving a model rocket ship in one hand and a toy football in the other. "TA-DA!" He wore nothing except his favorite Squidboy underpants and a set of fake teeth that used to be part of a Halloween costume. Iggy calls them his "spider teeth" because they're decorated with a fake plastic spider.

Iggy is weird that way; he's almost always either practically naked or wearing a costume.

"Look, Dano!" Iggy said, pointing to his mouth. "Spider teef!"

"Iggy, you aren't allowed to touch my Planet Blaster stuff, okay?"

"Okay, Dano," he said, smiling. Even I have to admit that Iggy's a pretty cute kid when he smiles.

But then Iggy started climbing the ladder up to my top bunk, and the cuteness ended.

·3·

THE GOBBLEBOX

CRASH!

WITHIN A SECOND, Iggy had climbed up to the top bunk and grabbed my favorite Planet Blaster spaceship—the Vortex Chariot. I tried to snatch it away from him, but his grip was surprisingly strong. Iggy pulled. I tugged harder. Finally we both fell backward, and the Vortex Chariot broke apart and fell to the floor. We stared down at it where it lay on the ground.

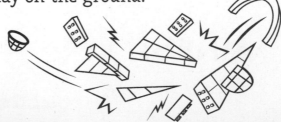

"Now look what you did!" I yelled. "You're not even supposed to be up here on the top bunk!"

"YOU bwoke it!" Iggy shouted back.

"I told you: Don't touch ANY of them EVER!" I shook my pillow out of its pillowcase, then used the empty sack to store all the Planet Blaster models I could grab. I wedged the bulky, toy-stuffed pillowcase between my back and the wall.

"Give me!! Dat MINES!!!"

I leaned back, trying to keep the pillow-case out of Iggy's reach. In the process, I accidentally crushed a couple more of the models. "No, Iggy, they're *mine*. Anyway, there's no such word as 'mines.'"

"Here," I said. "You can have *this*." I picked up a babyish looking plastic car—a lame one I haven't played with in years—and offered it to Iggy as a substitute.

Iggy's face turned red and blotchy, which meant that a scream was getting ready to blow like lava bursting out of a volcano. *Uh-oh*, I thought. *The longer the quiet, blotchy face, the louder the scream.*

I covered my ears and braced myself for the worst tantrum in history. Finally it burst out.

"*NOOOOOOOOOOOOO!!!!!!!!!!!!!!!*" Iggy threw the car over the bed railings and dove for my pillowcase filled with Planet Blaster models.

I managed to throw the pillowcase off the bed just before Iggy could grab it. Unfortunately, my dad happened to walk into the room at that exact moment, and the plastic-filled pillowcase clobbered him in the face.

Iggy howled. I tried to hide under my blankets to block out the noise.

My mom rushed into the room carrying two bags of frozen vegetables. She pressed a bag of frozen peas against Iggy's hand and gave my dad a bag of frozen carrots for his cheek. That's one of the weird things about my mom: When people get hurt, she gives them frozen vegetables instead of an ice cube or a Band-Aid. "That will help keep the swelling down," she explained.

Then Mom spoke in her big-trouble voice: "Daniel and Iggy!! Sharing a room means sharing toys and taking turns without fighting. And since these toys are causing trouble right now, they are going into the Gobblebox until the two of you find a way to get along."

"Nooooo!" Iggy and I both cried. "Not the GOBBLEBOX!"

The "Gobblebox" is where my parents hide our toys when we're in trouble. When I was younger, I used to be scared of the Gobblebox, because my parents acted so mysterious when they talked about it.

"What does it LOOK like?" I would ask.

"The Gobblebox can be as big or small as it needs to be," my dad would say. "It eats toys of all sizes when children misbehave."

"But where IS it?"

"It can be anyplace it wants to be," my mom would say.

Now that I'm older, I know that the Gobblebox is just some cardboard box in the house where my parents hide toys until Iggy and I earn them back by being good. On the other hand, if I think about it too much, I can still get a little freaked out about the idea of a box that lives in my house and eats my toys.

Thanks a lot, Iggy, I thought as I watched my mom and dad leave with all my favorite stuff. It was only my first day sharing a room with Iggy, and I had already lost my favorite Planet Blaster models.

I guess things can't get any worse than they are now, I thought.

Unfortunately, I was completely wrong. As it turned out, things could get much, much worse.

CHAUNCEY MORBYD

MOM SAID IT WAS TIME for Iggy to take a nap in what *used* to be my bed, so I left him alone. I stood in the front room, just staring out the window and trying to decide what to do next. I wasn't in the mood to read a book or play with my friend Chauncey Morbyd, who lives down the street. Instead, I watched the new kid, whose family had just moved into the house next door.

The new kid seemed to be very into gar-

dening because he was outside with shovels and rakes and some other strange-looking tools that I guessed were for planting flowers or vegetables.

I thought about going over there to introduce myself, but I'm kind of shy about meeting new people. I mean, I'm not the type to just go up to a complete stranger and introduce myself out of the blue with a bunch of pleased-to-meet-you stuff.

Just then, the doorbell rang, so I jumped up to answer it. I knew it would be Chauncey Morbyd. He usually comes over to my house at least once a day to look for a decent snack since his mom doesn't let him eat any sugar.

It turned out I was right.

"Do you have any gum?" Chauncey asked, after I opened the door.

"I'm not sure," I said. "I don't think so."

"Can you ask your mom?" Chauncey walked right into the house. He never waits to be invited, which really bugs my parents.

My mom was downstairs in the basement doing laundry. I didn't feel like walking all the way down there, so I opened the door and shouted down the basement steps: "MOM— DO WE HAVE ANY GUM?"

"NO!" was the answer.

"She said no," I told Chauncey.

"Can you ask your dad?"

"He isn't here; he just left to take Dottie to a playdate."

Chauncey spied my mom's purse and rummaged through it, looking for chewing gum.

"Cut it out!" I whispered. "We'll get in trouble."

"Ha!" Chauncey held up a dirty, smushed stick of gum from the bottom of Mom's purse. "She *does* have gum!"

I heard a creaking sound and turned to see Iggy peering out at us through a crack in the doorway. When he saw Chauncey, he ran out of the bedroom: "HEY, CHAUNCEY! I A BIG BOY NOW! I SWEEP IN DANO'S BIG-BOY BED!"

"Hey, Iggy!" Chauncey leaned close to Iggy, as if he was about to tell him a big, juicy secret. "Remember that bag of old Halloween candy in your room? Do you still have it?"

Iggy and Dottie both have secret stashes of very old Halloween candy, and each time he comes over, Chauncey makes them give him some.

Iggy shook his head. "Mom throw it away. But I know where Mom hided some marsho-wowows!"

Chauncey turned to me: "Huh? What are 'marsho-wowows'?"

"He means marshmallows," I said.

Iggy climbed up on the kitchen counter and opened a cabinet, where Mom kept some stale, multicolored marshmallows. They were old and hard as rocks, but Iggy and Chauncey didn't seem to mind. They both stuffed a couple handfuls into their mouths. Chauncey even stashed extra marshmallows in his pockets to save for later.

My mom always says that eating candy gives Iggy the "sugar crazies." She might have a point because a minute later, Iggy and Chauncey were running around the house, playing a game called "Squidboy Fights the Blue Freaks." I figured I might as well join them, so I started running around, too.

I don't recommend trying this at home unless you have the really sturdy type of little brother, but here's how you play Squidboy Fights the Blue Freaks, in case you're wondering:

Playing Squidboy Fights the Blue Freaks with Iggy is usually pretty fun, but this time Iggy kicked me in the face when I jumped on him.

"Ow!" I yelled. I sat on Iggy a little harder than usual to punish him and, just my luck, that was the moment my mom walked into the room to see what all the yelling was about.

When he saw Mom, Iggy started crying just to get me in trouble.

And just my luck again, Mom happened to look at the carpet and see a wad of pink chewing gum—gum that must have fallen out of Chauncey's mouth.

"Who left GUM on the floor?!" Mom demanded.

"Not me, Mrs. Loomis," Chauncey lied. "My mom says gum is bad for my teeth. It must be Daniel's gum."

"It is NOT my gum, and you know it!"

That's the trouble with Chauncey. Whenever he comes over, I always get in trouble.

Mom said it was time for Chauncey to go home since the three of us weren't playing nicely.

That was fine with me; I didn't appreciate Chauncey getting me in trouble, and I wasn't in the mood to play another game of Squidboy Fights the Blue Freaks either.

"Iggy, go back to your nap," said Mom.

"NEVER!!" Iggy yelled.

Mom took Iggy by the hand and dragged him back to my bedroom.

After Chauncey left, I went back to my seat at the front window and noticed that the new kid was still outside in his front yard. He stared at something on the ground, as if he had just discovered the most amazing thing he'd ever seen in his life. He bent down to examine whatever it was through some kind of tool that looked like a little microscope. I watched as he put things in little bags and boxes.

I had never seen anyone act so interested in his own front yard before, and watching him made me curious. In fact, I was so curious that I forgot to feel shy. Plus, I figured this was my chance to introduce myself without Iggy around to embarrass me.

I decided to just walk right up to this new kid and find out what he was up to.

· 5 ·

THE NEW KID

"HI, DANIEL," said the new kid, before I had even opened my mouth to say hello.

"How do you know my name?"

"Oh, your parents told my parents that the two of us should hang out sometime," he explained. "I'm Alistair." He stuck out his hand, so I shook it.

I thought the formal handshake was a little weird for a kid his age. I also noticed that Alistair wore a cool-looking watch that was

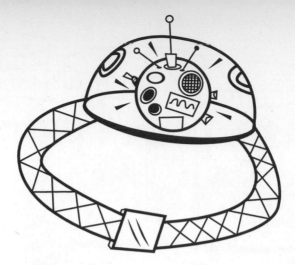

different from any watch I had seen before. It was loaded with so many round screens and tiny buttons, it reminded me of a tiny spaceship on his wrist.

Alistair's face, on the other hand, seemed familiar. I felt sure that I recognized him from someplace.

I know this new kid from somewhere! I kept thinking. *But from where?*

Alistair showed me a collection of insects he had trapped in little bug-catching containers: all kinds of caterpillars, beetles, ladybugs, spiders, and butterflies. It was pretty interesting because Alistair had a few species I had never even noticed around my yard.

"What are you going to do with them?" I asked.

"Just the usual," he shrugged. "Observe them, take notes, do some molecular and genetic analysis."

"Molecular and genetic analysis" sounded pretty cool, even though I wasn't really sure what it meant. I noticed that one of the containers held some weird-looking tubes filled with something that looked like clear Jell-O in different colors; the whole thing looked like a miniature science lab. Some of the tubes contained live bugs; others contained dead bugs and other weird objects suspended in the colorful jiggly stuff. I noticed one tube that contained something *really* strange. It looked like it might be some type of sea creature's tentacle.

"What's *that*?" I asked, pointing. I tried to get a closer look, but Alistair quickly grabbed all the containers and hid them in a backpack that rested on the front porch. "I shouldn't leave those sitting out in the sun," he said. "I use the containers to preserve insects for dissection and to study their DNA."

I must have looked confused because Alistair started teaching me about DNA: "It's kind of like a secret code that's inside every cell of every living creature," Alistair said. "DNA tells the cell what type of proteins to make; it's like a set of instructions telling the cell what it's supposed to be doing in the body."

"I know what DNA is," I said. To be honest, I had forgotten the details, but I remembered it had something to do with whether you end up tall or short and whether you have blue eyes or brown eyes and stuff like that.

Alistair shrugged. "Anyway, I'll probably let the living bugs go after I examine them for a few days." Alistair picked up a jar that contained a living grasshopper. "Here—do you want to take a look at *this* one?"

Alistair let me look at the grasshopper through a high-powered magnifying glass. Then he showed me how to find and catch a little cricket and store it in one of his bug-catcher boxes.

Just then, I glanced up and spotted Chauncey outside in his yard, a few houses down the street. He was just standing there, hitting a tree with a stick. I suddenly felt like hiding. *If Chauncey spots me and Alistair,* I thought, *he'll come over here and try to convince us to sneak back into my house and steal marshmallows, or wake up Iggy from his nap.* (Chauncey has a newborn baby sister and an older sister, but he says he'd rather play with

Iggy at my house. Why? Because it's so fun to roll Iggy up in a blanket and sit on him.)

"Hey—" said Alistair, "do you want to come in and take a look at my Planet Blaster Technoblok models?"

It was like Alistair could read my mind. "Sure! Let's go right now!" I followed Alistair inside, feeling relieved to have a break from another afternoon with Chauncey. I also guessed that Alistair must have some pretty cool stuff inside his house.

And guess what? For once, I was completely right!

· 6 ·

PLANET BLASTERS

WELL, TO BE HONEST, the very *first* thing I noticed inside Alistair's house was a funny smell. I felt like I was sitting in front of a plate full of my most *unfavorite* cooked vegetables.

But when I saw Alistair's room, I forgot about the smell problem pretty fast. In fact, I knew that Alistair was definitely going to be my best friend for the whole rest of the school year no matter how bad his house smelled.

Why?

Because what I found in Alistair's room was the coolest collection of Planet Blaster stuff *I had ever seen in my entire life*. And believe me, I've seen a lot, because I've seen every Planet Blaster movie and built about half the Planet Blaster Technoblok spacecraft models that exist. *Everything* was there. He even had the very rare Sargonian Desolator and the Pyrokyte Transfixor.

I was in awe. "Did you build all of these?"

"Yes," he said. "You can have one of them if you like them."

"I CAN *HAVE* ONE OF THEM?!"

"Yes."

I stared at Alistair. Suddenly, I realized why he seemed so familiar. "Hey!" I blurted. "Now I know why I recognize you! You look like Zip Starwagon!"

"You mean, the boy in your favorite movie?"

I stared at Alistair. "How did you know that *Planet Blaster* is my favorite movie?"

"Oh, I just estimated, since you like the Planet Blaster toys."

"You 'estimated'?" Alistair had a strange way of talking.

"*Planet Blaster* is my favorite, too," he said.

It was true that Alistair's face resembled the only human character in my favorite *Planet Blaster* movie. I suddenly couldn't believe my luck as I looked around Alistair's room; I felt as if a bunch of my favorite shows and toys had just turned into a family and moved into the house next door.

"Keep the Desolator," said Alistair. "Since it's your favorite."

He was right; it was my favorite. "Are you *sure?*" I couldn't imagine giving away the Sargonian Desolator if it had belonged to me.

"Which Planet Blaster model is *your* favorite?" I asked.

Alistair tilted his head and looked around his bedroom. He didn't look very excited, considering how many amazing models he had in there.

If this were my room, I thought, *I would just sit in here all day and never come out.*

"They're all interesting," Alistair finally said, "but they're old-fashioned."

"Old-fashioned?" This comment didn't make any sense. How could space vessels that travel across galaxies seem "old-fashioned"?

"Um, I just meant that they aren't the new-

est models you can buy at the store," Alistair explained.

"What about that watch you're wearing?" I asked. "Is that old-fashioned, too?"

"This watch is the opposite of old-fashioned," said Alistair in a very serious voice. Then he did something surprising: He pointed his watch in the direction of one of his Planet Blaster models and pushed a button. The next thing I knew, the model spaceship was flying around the room! Just like magic, he had turned a Technoblok model into an amazing robot plane!

I just stood there with my mouth hanging

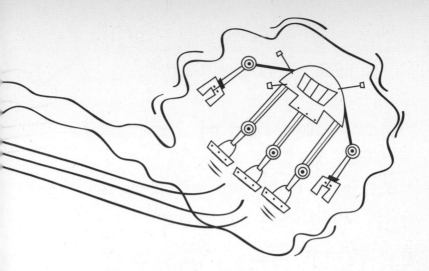

open as I watched. As far as I could tell, the model spaceship didn't have an engine or batteries, so how could it fly?

"Can I try that watch?" It was all I could do to keep myself from grabbing the watch from Alistair's wrist and pressing all the buttons.

"Well. . . . You have to be really careful with it. . . ."

I could tell Alistair didn't want to let me touch that amazing watch.

"It's not really a toy."

"Don't worry," I said. "I'll be careful."

"No—you have to be REALLY careful."

"Okay. I'll be REALLY careful."

"Don't push any random buttons."

"Why not?"

Alistair looked horrified. "What do you mean, 'Why not?'"

"Well, what do the other buttons *do*?" I worried that Alistair had changed his mind about letting me wear the watch.

"It would take too long to explain," said Alistair, "but believe me, you *don't* want to push the wrong button on this watch. We would both be in HUGE trouble."

I figured he must be worried that the aircraft would get out of control and blast through a window or something.

"Look," I said, "I promise I won't touch the other buttons. Just let me try it one time, okay?"

Alistair thought for a moment and then carefully removed the watch and placed it on my wrist. The watch felt heavier on my arm than I had expected.

Alistair showed me which button to push

as I pointed the watch in the direction of the Sargonian Desolator. A second later, I watched the little vehicle light up and silently lift itself from the floor.

Wow, wow, wow!! I thought. I was practically bouncing up and down with excitement because I had just been given a new Sargonian Desolator that could actually *fly* with the help of Alistair's amazing watch. I had a new friend whose room was filled with my favorite Planet Blaster stuff—a friend who knew how to build Technoblok models that could turn into robots of all kinds!

I decided Alistair was the most talented kid I had ever met. Even if he was a little odd.

·7·

THE BROCCOLI FARM

JUST MY LUCK! Right when I thought I was having the perfect afternoon with Alistair, I looked up and saw a pair of binoculars peering at us through the window. The boy behind the binoculars had tried to disguise himself with a fake beard and mustache, but I could tell right away that it was Chauncey.

Chauncey owns night-vision goggles, high-powered binoculars, and disguises, but playing spy games with him is never fun because

he won't share any of his cool spy gear. Besides, he only spies on people who *already know he's watching them* and who wish he would just leave them alone. What Chauncey enjoys most about spying is making other people mad.

I explained to Alistair that it was best to just ignore Chauncey. That was pretty difficult, though, because Chauncey kept knocking on the window.

The next time I looked up, Chauncey was gone, so I figured he had finally given up spying and decided to go home.

But then Alistair's mother came into the room.

Look who I found outside! Another friend for you, Alistair!

Well, I think Alistair's mom realized her mistake pretty fast, because Chauncey has no manners about meeting new people.

I think it smells nice!

What REEKS in this HOUSE?! It smells like baby poop, or rotten BROCCOLI or something GROSS!!

That must be the broccoli soup I'm cooking.

Look, I didn't like the cooked-vegetable smell either, but I wasn't about to risk hurting Alistair's feelings when he owned the best collection of Planet Blaster stuff in the entire neighborhood. Besides, I had kind of gotten used to the smell, so I didn't notice it that much any more.

Alistair explained that his family has to eat a lot of broccoli because they all have a very unusual food allergy. "In fact," he said, "broccoli is practically the only food my body is able to digest."

Chauncey looked like he was about to have a heart attack. "You mean, you can't eat ANYTHING else?!" he practically yelled. "ONLY BROCCOLI?!"

I knew what Chauncey was thinking: *Forget about getting any good snacks at Alistair's house.*

"Not very much of anything else," said Alistair. "Approximately ninety-five percent of the food I eat is some form of broccoli."

"You're lying," said Chauncey. "Nobody could eat that much broccoli and still be alive.

Alistair took us to his kitchen and opened the refrigerator door.

It did sound pretty awful to have nothing but broccoli on your plate at every meal. On the other hand, Alistair didn't seem to feel the least bit sorry for himself. *Maybe he just really likes broccoli,* I thought.

"Look," Alistair said, pointing. Through the kitchen window, we saw that Alistair's backyard looked like a little farm. "That's our broccoli garden."

"That's gonna be a lot of broccoli," said Chauncey.

"Let's hope," said Alistair. "The soil in this yard has a perfect pH of 6.8 and lots of organic matter, so it's really ideal for growing broccoli."

Chauncey and I stared at Alistair as if he had just turned into a broccoli plant himself. I had never met a kid who knew so much about growing broccoli; that's for sure.

"Remind me NOT to come to your birthday party when it's time to eat the broccoli cake," said Chauncey.

"Okay," said Alistair. "I'll remind you."

I had a feeling Alistair actually *liked* broccoli cake.

"So what else is there to do around this vegetable dump?" Chauncey asked.

We went into Alistair's room, and I could tell that Chauncey was impressed with Alistair's Planet Blaster Technoblok models and robots, even though he wouldn't admit it. It bugged me that Chauncey kept saying things like, "My room is actually bigger than this room," and "Oh, I already have that one."

I wanted Chauncey to see that Alistair's models were actually way cooler than anything at Chauncey's house. "Hey, Alistair," I said, "you should show Chauncey how you can turn the models into flying robots with your watch!"

"What watch?" Chauncey asked.

Then I saw that Alistair wasn't wearing his watch anymore. "Hey, where's your remote-control watch?"

"What remote-control watch?!" Chauncey demanded.

"Oh, I think the batteries are running out. It stopped working so I took it off."

Somehow I doubted that this was true. "I

might have some extra batteries at my house," I offered.

"It takes a special type of battery," said Alistair. "You wouldn't have it at your house."

I guessed the truth was that Alistair didn't want Chauncey to play with his special watch. I couldn't blame him, since Chauncey would be likely to press every button without asking first. Still, I was disappointed.

"We can still build Technoblok models," said Alistair.

"I'm bored," said Chauncey, after we had worked on building models for about half a minute.

"Why?" Alistair asked.

"Because this is so BORING! Right, Daniel?"

"I'm not bored." I was kind of hoping Chauncey would just leave and go home.

"Let's play hide-and-seek," said Chauncey.

"Let's not." Hide-and-seek is another one of Chauncey's favorite games, and he always picks really frustrating hiding places. One time when we were playing hide-and-seek, Chauncey went all the way to his grandmother's house a few blocks away, and hid up in her attic.

I finally got so sick of looking for Chauncey that I went back home to watch TV.

"The rule is that the guest gets first choice," said Chauncey. "I'm the guest, and I pick hide-and-seek."

"But I'm also Alistair's guest," I replied, "and my choice is building Technobloks."

"But I'm his *newest* guest," Chauncey argued. "You've been here for HOURS. I mean, you practically *LIVE* here by now."

We heard a high-pitched giggle. It was Alistair.

"What's so funny?" Chauncey demanded.

"I don't know!" Alistair just as surprised by his own laughter as we were. He stared at Chauncey and me for a moment, then burst into a new fit of giggles. It was as if he had suddenly turned into a much younger kid. "I'm sorry," Alistair gasped. "The two of you are just so *strange!*"

Chauncey and I stared at Alistair. Why was he calling *us* strange? You would have thought Alistair was watching the most hilarious movie in the world from the way he acted.

"I can't stop!" Alistair rolled on the ground, clutching his stomach. "This feels so weird—*laughing!*"

"Okay, I've had enough of this place," said Chauncey. "Come on, Daniel. Let's go back to your house."

"I'm staying," I said. Even with Alistair acting so weird, I knew I would rather keep building Technobloks right where I was than play with Chauncey and Iggy at my house. *And maybe if Chauncey leaves,* I thought, *Alistair will put his watch back on so we can make these vehicles fly again.* Chauncey didn't like that. "Aren't you supposed to be grounded, Daniel?"

"No."

"Does your mom even know you're playing over here?"

"Yes." (She actually didn't, but I figured she wouldn't mind.)

"I'm leaving," said Chauncey, still hoping that I would follow him.

"Bye," I said.

Alistair fell silent for a moment. He sat up and looked at Chauncey walking out the door and then burst into a laughing fit all over again.

After Chauncey left, I kept working on Technobloks. I figured Alistair would eventually stop his crazy giggling and that things would go back to normal.

8

THE HUGE MISTAKE

ALISTAIR EVENTUALLY stopped giggling, but unfortunately for me, he also decided that he was tired of building Technobloks in his room. "Can't we go to *your* house now?" he asked.

I tried to explain to Alistair that my mom had just put all my cool toys away as a punishment for fighting with my little brother, who might still be taking a nap in what used to be my room. But this only seemed to make

Alistair *more* interested in going to my house.

"I want to meet your little brother and sister," he said.

This seemed pretty weird to me. But I guessed that I had to be nice about it if I wanted to be invited back to Alistair's house again.

"Sure, I guess we can go play at my house," I sighed. *So much for my afternoon escape from Iggy,* I thought.

As we crossed the front lawn, heading toward my house, Alistair paused to pick up a dead bug that looked like a gigantic fly with bulging eyes.

"It's a cicada," he said. "They live underground for seventeen years. Then they come out, climb up a tree, and start singing to attract a mate. Hear that buzzing sound in the trees?"

The trees had started making a weird, buzzing sound a few days ago, but I had gotten so used to it, I didn't really notice it any-more.

"That's the sound of cicadas." Alistair un-zipped his backpack and dropped the dead cicada into one of those jelly-filled tube-containers.

"Why do you keep so many dead bugs in there?" I asked. I wished Alistair would let me take a closer look; he seemed pretty secretive about the little containers in his backpack.

"I put each one in a special substance that separates out some of the bug's DNA. That way I can study the bug's genetic code," Alistair said.

"Huh." I kind of knew what he meant, sort of.

"DNA is what determines whether you be-come a plant, a bug, an animal, or a person. Change the DNA code and you might get a whole new creature."

My mom greeted us as we walked through the front door. I had a feeling she would ask

Alistair about a hundred questions, since he was new in the neighborhood, and I was right.

Alistair suddenly acted as if he had been brought down to the police station for questioning. Nobody likes answering my mom's boring questions about school, but Alistair seemed weirdly *surprised* by them. I got the feeling he had never even *thought* about going to school before.

Then Alistair made a sudden announcement: "I'll go to Daniel's school tomorrow!"

If you ask me, it sounded as if he had just now made that decision. "I'll be in Daniel's class," he added.

This seemed to make my mom happy. "Oh, how nice!" she said.

"Are we free to go now, Mom?" I asked.

"Of course," said Mom. "And Alistair, I'll invite your parents over for coffee sometime soon."

"I don't think they can drink coffee," Alistair said. "For health reasons."

"Can they drink tea?"

"Well . . ."

I was worried that Alistair would start talking about his family's broccoli diet, which might give my mom ideas about replacing some of my favorite foods with vegetables. I needed to get him out of there fast. "Come on, Alistair," I said. "Let's go to my room."

"Oh, Daniel," Mom said, "can you and

Alistair keep an eye on Iggy and Dottie while I get dinner ready?"

I sighed. "Can't Dad watch them?"

"Dad is having his 'Quiet Time' in the bathroom."

When my dad has Quiet Time in the bathroom, we don't see him for a while. He says a locked bathroom is the only place in the house where he can hear himself think.

Just then, Iggy and Dottie burst through Dottie's bedroom door and ran toward Alistair. The two of them were so excited to meet Alistair, you would have thought Santa Claus himself had come to visit our house.

Before I could steer Alistair away, Iggy and Dottie dragged him into Dottie's room to show off their babyish toys.

I figured Alistair would get bored with that stuff pretty quickly. Instead, he acted weirdly *interested* in everything Iggy and  Dottie showed him. I mean, you would have thought he had never seen stuffed animals and dolls before. Alistar listened to Iggy's completely dumb and wrong descriptions of cartoon characters like Squidboy, the Blue Freaks, and a made-up character called "Pinkie Horse" that Iggy and Dottie invented.

Alistair listened to Dottie's descriptions of her "booful party dresses" her "booful dollhouse," and her "twirlie-twirl balloring tutus."

Iggy showed Alistair his collection of superhero underpants.

Iggy and Dottie climbed on Alistair's back for a horsey ride.

It seemed like Alistair was never going to get tired of playing with Iggy and Dottie! I needed to think of something to distract him.

Just then, my mom peeked into the room. "Thanks for playing so nicely together, everyone! I just need to run to a neighbor's house to borrow an egg for a recipe I'm making. Daniel and Alistair, can you make sure everyone behaves for a couple minutes until I get back?"

"Sure, Mom," I said.

I suddenly realized that I had a great opportunity: With Mom out of the house and Dad having his bathroom Quiet Time, I had the perfect chance to sneak a few toys from the Gobblebox without anyone noticing. *If I show Alistair my awesome Planet Blaster stuff, I thought, he'll lose interest in Iggy and Dottie pretty fast.*

"Pssst—Alistair!" I whispered. "Follow me; I want to show you something!"

"I'll be right back," Alistair told Dottie and Iggy, who were still busy entertaining him with their fascinating objects. I guessed the two of them had never met anyone who found them so interesting before.

"Come on," I whispered, leading Alistair upstairs, toward my parents' bedroom. I figured the Gobblebox was in my mom's closet, exactly where she always hides it. "I'll show you the Gobblebox."

"What's a Gobblebox?" Alistair asked.

I told him it was the place my parents hide our toys when we get in trouble. "We can sneak some Technobloks out of the Gobblebox," I said, "and then you can help me build one of those cool robots."

We tiptoed into my parents' room and turned on the light. The first thing we discovered was a big mess. It's kind of funny that my parents have a messy room, because when a messy room belongs to a kid, it suddenly drives them crazy. Everywhere I looked, I saw piles of dirty socks.

"I bet the Gobblebox is in Mom's closet," I whispered. "That's usually where she hides stuff."

Alistair nodded.

When I pushed open my mom's closet door, we both froze.

Mom had used a felt-tip marker to decorate the box with sharp teeth and an evil smile.

Just as I reached into the box to grab one of my favorite Planet Blaster models, I heard Dottie yelling downstairs: "IGGY! WHAT YOU DO DAT FOR! DAT SO MESSY AND GWOSS!"

Uh-oh, I thought. *What have they done now?*

"My research equipment!" Alistair turned and ran from the room.

I followed Alistair down the stairs and back into Dottie's bedroom.

Alistair and I just stared. Because what we discovered in that room wasn't pretty.

9

BUG CANDY

IGGY SAT ON THE FLOOR holding a bunch of dead bugs in his hand, including the big cicada Alistair had found in my yard. There were empty tubes and glass containers all around him on the floor. Worst of all, his face and hair were covered with sticky, multicolored jelly—the weird-looking substance Alistair used to extract DNA from bugs. A ladybug, a fly, a centipede, and a bunch of other squished bugs were stuck in the gluey stuff on Iggy's cheeks.

"Taste YUCKY!" Iggy said.

Alistair looked pale as he pulled a cloth from his backpack and toweled off Iggy's face. He pried the slimy, dead bugs from Iggy's fist and put them in a container. "Did you put any of these bugs in your *mouth*, Iggy?" Alistair asked.

"No," said Iggy, "just da *bug candy*."

Alistair looked like he might faint. "'*Bug candy*'??"

"That isn't candy, Iggy!" I said. "How many times have Mom and Dad told you not to put stuff you find in your mouth? And you aren't supposed to open other people's backpacks, either."

"It *look* like bug candy," Iggy said. "Like when Mom made dat Jell-O wif bugs!"

Now I remembered what Iggy was talking about. Last Halloween, my mom made green and orange Jell-O with gummy worms and other candy bugs floating inside. It was one of the best desserts she's ever made. I could sort of understand why Iggy thought the chemical-covered bugs in Alistair's backpack might taste like  Jell-O or gummy worms. But still. *How could a kid get in so much trouble in only two minutes?*

Mom will be so mad at me, I thought, remembering how she had asked us to "keep an eye on Iggy and Dottie." *And she would be especially mad if she knew I was upstairs trying to sneak toys from the Gobblebox right when Iggy was eating bugs.*

But maybe she doesn't need to know, I thought. *Maybe Iggy is fine, and we can keep this little mistake secret.*

Alistair rushed around the room putting the lids back on his jars and tubes. He kept pointing to different containers and asking

Iggy about them: "Did you put *this* one in your mouth?"

Iggy nodded yes. "Dat one yucky."

"How about *this* one?"

"Yup! Dat one *super-duper* yuck-o!"

Each time Iggy said, yes, Alistair looked more worried. I worried, too. What if Iggy had been poisoned? In that case, I would be in HUGE trouble. We'd have to take Iggy to the emergency room, and then my parents would definitely find out that I had been sneaking upstairs.

"Do you think he needs to go to a doctor?" I whispered to Alistair. "Should I get my mom?"

We both looked at Iggy. He certainly *looked* fine. In fact, he looked healthier than ever.

"The stuff he ingested isn't toxic," said Alistair. "Although there might be some unpredictable effects."

"'Unpredictable' sounds bad," I said.

Alistair walked over to Iggy and looked

at him more closely. "Open your mouth, Iggy," he said.

Iggy opened his slimy, bug-stained mouth for Alistair and stuck out his tongue, which looked very gross with bits of insect legs and wings stuck to it.

Alistair didn't seem to mind how gross Iggy's tongue looked. He just pushed a button on his watch and shone a beam of blue light into Iggy's mouth. Then he flipped open a little dome on his watch and began pressing a bunch of buttons very quickly as if he were typing a message.

"Alistair, what are you *doing*?" I asked.

"I'm checking some data. The good news is that Iggy seems to be fine. At least for the moment."

"How do you *know*? Alistair, it's cool that your watch has a flashlight, but you're not a doctor, and—"

"We don't need to panic, Daniel. I'll fix this."

"Fix what?"

"I'll explain tomorrow. Now I have to go back to my house to make a few calls." Alistair quickly gathered his belongings and hurried out the door.

Then he paused and walked back to me more slowly. "Daniel, don't tell your parents about this, okay?"

The last thing I wanted to do was tell my mom what happened. But what if Alistair had no idea what he was talking about? What if Iggy was actually *not* okay?!

"I *promise* he'll be okay," said Alistair, sensing my worries.

I *wanted* to believe Alistair. "Okay," I said. "But if Iggy starts acting sick, then I'll have to tell them."

"Okay," said Alistair. "Good!" He hurried

down the front steps just as my mom returned from the neighbor's house, carrying an egg.

"Leaving already, Alistair?" Mom asked. "Are you and Daniel going to walk to school together tomorrow?"

"School?" Alistair paused on the sidewalk, looking confused. "Oh, yes. *School*. Daniel, I will see you tomorrow to walk to school!"

I watched Alistair hurry back to his house. Was this new kid a genius and a great new friend? Or was he completely crazy?

And how worried should I be about Iggy?

·10·

A RUDE AWAKENING

I WATCHED IGGY all through dinner, looking for signs that he might be sick after eating that bug-DNA serum. *If something looks wrong, I told myself, I'll tell Mom and Dad what happened, even if it means getting in trouble.*

I noticed that Iggy ate lots of vegetables without even being told, but other than that, he seemed fine.

By bedtime, I had pretty much decided there was nothing to worry about.

I was lying in bed in the dark, reading a Squidboy comic book with my flashlight when Iggy suddenly bounced up into the top bunk next to me.

He startled me; I wasn't used to seeing him in my room at night yet. I also suddenly had the eerie feeling that Iggy had actually jumped into my bed *without using the ladder.*

But that's impossible, I thought. *My bed is at least five feet off the ground, so there's no way Iggy could get up here without the ladder.* Then I reminded myself that I should be re-lieved that Iggy is strong and healthy after eating Alistair's bugs earlier in the day. *That was a close one,* I told myself.

"Hi, Dano," said Iggy, putting his face close to mine. He wore one of Dottie's Cinderella nightgowns, and also had a pacifier in his mouth.

He grinned and pointed at Dottie's night-gown: "Look, Dano! Cinderella!"

"Cinderella isn't even cool, Iggy." Iggy still

doesn't get the basic fact that some clothes are for girls and some are for boys. He's also not supposed to suck on his pacifier anymore, but he hides them in secret places, like under furniture. Every time Mom takes one away, he finds a replacement.

"Squidboy!" Iggy shouted when he saw my comic book. "Cool!"

Iggy crawled under the covers next to me, and we looked at the *Squidboy* comic book together. He smelled like baby shampoo and his pacifier made a *squeak, squeak, squeak* sound that was weirdly comforting. I admit it: it actually felt kind of nice having him curl up next to me—like having a soft little animal sleep on my bed.

Maybe that's the key to sharing a room with Iggy, I thought. *I'll just pretend he's my pet. I'll pretend he's a new breed of animal that's part dog and part kangaroo.*

I must have fallen asleep because the next thing I knew, I awoke to the strange feeling of something on my body—something warm and wet.

I realized that Iggy had wet the bed. "Ewww! Wake up, Iggy!"

Iggy sat up. "I need to go potty."

"MOM! IGGY PEED IN MY BED!"

A minute later, my mom and dad came into my room with their puffy middle-of-the-night faces. My dad took Iggy into the bathroom. My mom changed the sheets on my bed while I changed my pajamas.

"I can't believe Iggy peed on me!" I complained.

"It probably happened because he isn't used to being in a new bed," said my mom. "It was an accident, so don't make him feel bad, okay?"

What about MY feelings? I thought. In one day, I had gone from a boy who had a bunch of cool Planet Blaster stuff in his bedroom to a pee-soaked boy with *nothing* in his room. Nothing except a baby roommate named Iggy.

I climbed back into bed and listened to my

parents trying to convince Iggy that it was time to go back to bed, and not yet time for "bweakfast."

"You can't wear that, Iggy; you peed on it."

"I want wear it!"

"How about your Squidboy PJs?"

"I want CINDERELLA!"

As my mother and Iggy argued about whether Iggy could keep wearing Dottie's Cinderella nightgown, I lay in bed and worried about my life with Iggy. *If Iggy is going to be my pet,* I thought, *maybe his bed should be a pile of newspapers in the corner. Better yet: maybe Dad could build a little "Iggy house" outside, in the backyard.*

"NO DIAPER!" Iggy screamed. "I big boy!"

"I know, honey, but you just went pee-pee in your bed." Now Mom was trying to convince Iggy to wear a pull-up diaper "for extra nighttime protection."

"No diaper!" Iggy insisted. "I sleep naked."

"Stop it, Iggy! Here—put your Squidboy underpants *over* the diaper. Now you still look like a big kid," said Mom.

Iggy shuffled back toward our bunk bed, wearing his pull-up diaper covered by Squidboy underpants, and dragging his favorite snow-bunny blanket on the floor behind him.

Was it my imagination, or was Iggy taller than he had been just a few hours earlier?

"Good night, sweetie." My mother kissed Iggy and tucked him into the lower bunk bed.

"Good night, Daniel."

Mom reached into the top bunk to straighten my covers.

"Um, can I have my toys back, Mom?"

"You know the rules about the Gobblebox, Daniel."

"Isn't getting *peed* on punishment enough?"

"You'll get the toys back when you and Iggy are ready to share. And I'm sure you'll both do better tomorrow."

I hoped she was right, but I wasn't so sure. For some reason, I had the feeling that something very strange was about to happen to Iggy and me.

·11·

DANIEL'S NIGHTMARE

I n my night-
mare, Iggy
grew so big that
the entire bunk
bed came crashing to
the ground. We were trapped in the bedroom
because Giant Iggy was too big to fit through
the doorway. He blocked my only escape from
the room.

I look up at Iggy's pudgy face. He was chewing on something.

Giant Iggy didn't answer. Instead he swallowed.

It was a little scary looking up at him. His chubby hands were the size of pillows.

Iggy grabbed a handful of my Technobloks and stuffed them into his mouth as if they were potato chips. He chewed them with a crunching sound.

Iggy reached down
with his chubby hand
and grabbed me. He
laughed as I strug-
gled to escape from
his grip. I tried to
kick his fingers,
which were now
the size of base-
ball bats, but he

only grinned. I screamed as Iggy lifted me higher and higher, toward his massive baby teeth.

I woke to the sound of Iggy calling for Mom and Dad and screaming about "squid monsters." My mom came into the bedroom to comfort him.

"It was just a dream, Iggy," Mom said. "There's no such thing as a squid monster— especially here in this house. You're safe. Now go back to sleep."

That was really weird, I thought, *because I just had a bad dream about a monster, too.*

Except in my dream, the monster was Iggy.

· 12 ·

UNDERPANTS AND OVERPANTS

THE NEXT MORNING, Iggy slept late and woke up grouchy. It's pretty unusual for him to wake up in a bad mood. Even on school days, he usually bounces out of bed with so much energy, you'd think he was heading off to see the circus instead of driving to preschool in a minivan.

But this time, Iggy sat at the breakfast table and glared at his bowl of cereal.

"Have a bite of cereal, Iggy," said Dad.

"*No.*"

"Just one bite?"

Iggy stuck his face in his cereal bowl and tried to lap up the milk like a dog.

"Okay, Mister, I think you're done with breakfast," said Mom.

Iggy screamed as Mom took away his cereal bowl.

"Somebody didn't sleep very well last night," said Mom. "Did Iggy have a bad dream?"

Iggy nodded. "I have a bery bad dweam!

"I dweam dat a squid monster gwab-ded me!

"And den I turn into a monster wif bug-wings and gwoss blobzees!

"And den Dano won't play wif me, and so I squish-ted him and sting-ded him!"

I felt a little queasy when I suddenly remembered my own bad dream: the nightmare that Iggy had turned into a giant creature that was large and strong enough to devour me. It seemed pretty weird that *both* Iggy and I had nightmares about Iggy turning into a monster. Maybe it was just a coincidence, but it gave me a bad feeling.

Was this what it would be like to sharing a room with Iggy from now on? A life of nightmares and midnight urine?

"Come on, Iggy and Dottie," said Mom. "You need to hurry up and get dressed."

For the next few minutes, Iggy and Dottie argued with Mom about what they were going to wear. Iggy wanted to wear his underpants *over* his jeans instead of under them. Dottie wanted to wear her princess nightgown instead of a regular dress or pants.

"Iggy," said Mom, "underpants go *under* your pants."

"But I want *SEE* Squidboy ON TOP my pants!" Iggy protested.

"Iggy," said Mom, "big boys wear *under-pants*, not *overpants*."

"BUT I WANT SEE DEM!!"

My mom gave up on Iggy and turned her attention to Dottie. "Dottie, honey, how about this pretty dress instead of the night-gown?"

"I HATE DAT ONE!" Dottie screeched. "I going step on it and weck it!"

My dad stood up from the table and chuck-led. As he walked to the sink, he made up a song called "I Never Knew It Could Be So Great!" which is about a jolly dad who's hav-ing a super-great time with his perfect kids. Dad's made-up songs happen to be my most unfavorite songs in the universe, but Dad keeps singing them.

Just then, I heard the doorbell ring, so I jumped up to open it. I found Alistair on our front porch, waiting to walk to school with me.

"Aren't you cold?" It was a surprisingly

chilly morning, but Alistair wasn't wearing a sweatshirt or jacket.

"I'm not cold," he said. "Are you?"

"Kind of." I shivered, and noticed that I could actually see my breath in the morning air. "I'd be freezing if I were *you*."

Alistair nodded. He didn't seem cold at all, and I noticed that I couldn't see *his* breath in the morning air.

Just as we started to head down the sidewalk, Iggy and Dottie burst through the front door.

"HEY, ALISTAIR!" they shouted, "WAIT FOR US!!" Dottie wore her nightgown, and Iggy wore his underpants over his jeans.

Alistair smiled when he saw them.

"IGGY—NO!" My dad followed them out the door, trying to herd Iggy and Dottie toward the van.

Iggy and Dottie are almost always late for school. Whenever it's time for them to leave, they run away, in two different directions.

"IGGY! DOTTIE! GET IN THE CAR!"

Iggy zipped right out of my dad's grasp. "I go wif Dano and Alistair!"

"IGGY! Come here! You're going to be late!"

"Get in the van, Iggy," I said. "Alistair and I are going to the school for big kids."

"I a big kid!"

My dad grabbed Iggy, but Iggy kicked and screamed. I was used to seeing Iggy act this way when he was angry. As Dad lifted Iggy and prepared to stuff him into his car seat, Iggy braced his feet against the side of the car and grabbed the car-door handle. Iggy had always been strong for his age, but he suddenly seemed *unusually* strong. And that's when something really, really strange happened: *Iggy ripped the car door off its hinges.*

·13·

THE SECRET

MY DAD STARED AT the car door lying on the ground and scratched his head. He looked pretty stunned. Pulling the door off a van was pretty extreme, even for Iggy.

Iggy's eyes grew wide. He wasn't yelling anymore; now he just looked scared.

"Poor, poor car," said Dottie. "Iggy bwoke it."

Dottie's comment made Iggy start bawling again, now louder than ever.

None of us could understand or explain

what had just happened. *Iggy just pulled a car door off its hinges,* I thought. *But that can't be possible, because he's just a little kid. So there must have been something wrong with car.*

Mom appeared on the front porch. "What happened? I heard something crash!"

Then Mom saw how Dad was just standing there, staring at the open side of the van where the door used to be, shaking his head.

"Oh, no!" Mom ran to the car to take a closer look. "See? I told you we needed to get that old thing into the shop!" said my mom. "That door has been acting weird for months."

"The door was making a weird *sound,*" said my dad. "It wasn't *falling off!*"

"Well, just look at it!" said my mom. "It certainly WAS falling off!"

"I could help you fix it," Alistair offered.

Based on what I had seen Alistair do with Technobloks, I figured he really might be able to fix the broken car door. "I bet Alistair could figure it out if you let him take a look, Dad," I

said. "He builds all kinds of vehicles and robots and stuff."

But my dad was in too bad a mood to even
give Alistair a chance. "Never mind," said
Dad. "I'll stop by the repair shop after I drop
off Iggy and Dottie. You guys just go to school
or you'll be late."

We all helped my dad move the car door
into the van. Then Alistair and I watched my
dad, Iggy, and Dottie drive away with the side
of the van wide open, as if they were riding
in some kind of delivery truck.

Iggy and Dottie laughed and waved to us
as they rode away with their hair blowing in
the cold breeze. The look on my dad's face
reminded me of the time I accidentally
stepped on his reading glasses just as he was
sitting down with his newspaper.

Alistair and I stared after them. "I was
afraid something like this might happen,"
Alistair said quickly.

I looked at him. "What do you mean?"

"Um—have you noticed anything strange about Iggy today?"

I thought this was kind of a dumb question since Alistair had just watched Iggy scream like a baboon, then pull a car door off its hinges, and ride away, giggling like a fool. "I guess it's strange for him to pull a car door off its hinges," I said, "but the car door must have been broken."

"Maybe," said Alistair, mysteriously. "Or maybe Iggy is actually *a lot stronger* today than he was yesterday."

"What are you talking about?"

"An ant, for example, can lift and carry a load up to fifty times its own body weight," said Alistair. "And I'm afraid that Iggy may have ingested more of that bug-DNA serum than I thought."

I stared at Alistair. "You think Iggy tore the door off a car because he ate bugs?!"

"Well, a combination of bugs and—"

"Alistair," I said, interrupting him, "everyone knows that eating a bug—or bug DNA—doesn't *turn you into* a bug. I mean, there are people who eat chocolate-covered ants, and they don't turn into superhuman ant people. Right?"

Alistair didn't answer. There was something he wasn't telling me.

"Alistair," I said, "you have to tell me what's going on."

Alistair paused on the sidewalk. "You have to promise to keep a secret," he whispered.

"Okay," I said. "I mean, depending on what it is."

Alistair swallowed. He looked nervous. "You're my only friend here," he said. "And I need to tell someone—"

"Tell someone *WHAT*?!" said a gruff voice

behind us. It was Chauncey; he had snuck up from behind.

I felt very annoyed to see Chauncey right when Alistair was about to spill the beans.

Chauncey put his arm around Alistair. "So what's the big secret?" he asked.

"Alistair was just telling me about his favorite secret broccoli recipes," I said.

"Ew," said Chauncey, backing away. "NO THANK YOU!"

"I'll tell you that *other* recipe later," Alistair said with a wink as we pushed through the front doors of our school and walked into the noisy crowd of kids in the hallway.

I sighed. I was dying to know what Alistair's secret was. How could I possibly concentrate on schoolwork with something like *this* on my mind?

· 14 ·

MR. BINNS

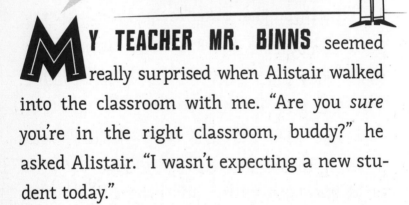

MY TEACHER MR. BINNS seemed really surprised when Alistair walked into the classroom with me. "Are you *sure* you're in the right classroom, buddy?" he asked Alistair. "I wasn't expecting a new student today."

Alistair showed Mr. Binns an official form that apparently was signed by someone in charge of the whole school system, so Mr. Binns told Alistair to find a spot for himself at my work group table.

I showed Alistair where to put his backpack and explained how our classroom is divided into different work groups who sit together. My team table was the "Orcas."

After taking attendance, Mr. Binns handed back some graded math quizzes.

I got a "sobbing face" grade because I had forgotten to put my name on the assignment. I used to feel really bad when I saw an unhappy or "mortally wounded" face on my assignments, but then I realized that Mr. Binns enjoys giving those faces more than the smiley ones because they're a lot more interesting for him to draw.

"What does *that* mean?" Alistair asked, pointing to the unhappy face on my paper.

I explained how, instead of regular grades like A or B or check-plus or check-minus, Mr. Binns gives us "face grades" so we

understand how the teacher *felt* when he was looking at our work.

Alistair still looked pretty confused, so I sketched a few of Mr. Binns's more popular face grades for him to use as a homework reference.

Chauncey leaned across the table to compare his math quiz grade with mine, like he always does. "I got more right than you," he said, pointing to the smiley face on his paper.

The Orcas table may have the most awesome work group name (which I chose), but the *down*side is that Chauncey also sits there. Chauncey has been moved to a lot of different tables because he drives people crazy by making annoying comments like, "You're not doing it right!" and "I got more right than you!" and "Why are you wearing THAT?!"

For a couple days, Chauncey even sat at Mr. Binns's desk, and I kept hearing Mr. Binns tell him, "Just THINK it, Chauncey; don't SAY it!"

Finally, Chauncey ended up at the Orcas table, next to lucky me.

And I had a feeling he was going to work extra hard to annoy me now that Alistair was also sitting with our work group.

·15·

ORCAS AND HAMSTERS

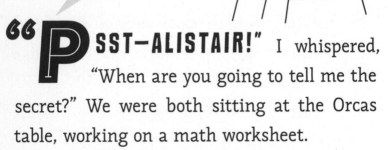

"**P**SST—ALISTAIR!**"** I whispered, "When are you going to tell me the secret?" We were both sitting at the Orcas table, working on a math worksheet.

"I can't tell you here," Alistair whispered. "I'll tell you later."

"*When?*" It was driving me crazy, wondering what this huge secret was.

"Soon," said Alistair, munching one of the broccoli florets he had brought with him in a little plastic bag. I had to admit that Alistair's interest in broccoli seemed a little weird to me, but I guessed that having a food allergy made broccoli pretty important to him.

Chauncey noticed Alistair's snack and raised his hand.

"Mr. Binns?"

"Yes, Chauncey?"

"Alistair is eating in the classroom."

"Alistair," said Mr. Binns, "the rule in our class is that we don't eat snacks during work time, unless you've brought double-fudge brownies for the teacher."

Alistair just stared at Mr. Binns. I could tell, he didn't get the joke.

"I was just kidding about the brownies," said Mr. Binns, "but no snacks right now, okay?"

And just like magic, Alistair reached into his backpack and produced another note signed by a doctor and also the school principal. I sneaked a peek and saw that this note said something about Alistair's "Special Dietary Needs in the Classroom."

Wow, I thought. *For someone who seemed confused about school, Alistair sure came prepared with plenty of excuse notes!*

"Okay, Alistair," said Mr. Binns, looking slightly annoyed, "but just keep the crunching sounds to a minimum."

"I'll try," said Alistair.

"Daniel, I expect both of you to turn your attention to the math worksheet I just gave you."

Alistair and I looked back at the math worksheet for a minute. I wondered if Alistair was confused, since he hadn't had much regular schooling.

"Why is Mr. Binns asking us these things?" Alistair whispered, pointing at his math worksheet.

"It's long division," I whispered back. "I can help you if you want."

"You mean," Alistair said, "Mr. Binns *doesn't know* these answers?!"

"Of course he does," I said. "He wants *us* to practice."

Alistair just shrugged and started writing.

When I looked over at him a moment later, I couldn't believe what I saw: Alistair had filled out the entire worksheet in an instant, while I had only completed two problems. I got the feeling he was getting *right* answers, too. Alistair put his paper aside and took some Technobloks out of his backpack.

"Alistair—what are you doing?!" Didn't Alistair know we weren't supposed to bring fun stuff like toys to school?

"I'm done with the assignment," he said. "Now I'll work on Technobloks."

I stared at him.

"Do you want me to do your math assignment for you?" Alistair asked. "That worksheet seems to be taking you a really long time."

I was still speechless. Alistair honestly didn't think there was anything wrong with doing my math assignment for me. *I* knew it was wrong, but I was also really sick of doing those long division problems.

"Okay," I whispered, "but don't let Mr. Binns or Chauncey see or we'll get in trouble."

Alistair started my math worksheet, and I started building Technobloks. I tried hard to hide the Technobloks, but it was no use. A minute later, Chauncey noticed and tattled.

"Mr. Binns," he said, "Daniel and Alistair brought toys into the classroom, which is distracting me from my work, and they're also copying each other's work."

That's when Mr. Binns moved me to the "Hamsters" table—the work group with the lamest name in the whole class. I sat there, squished between Christina, who talks nonstop, and Frankie, who spends a lot of time stabbing his paper with his pencil. (You have to be careful around Frankie, depending on his mood and the color shirt you're wearing. One wrong move when you're wearing orange, and you might end up with stab wounds on your arm.)

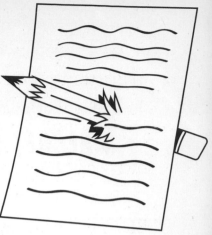

If Chauncey hadn't told on me, I'd still be at the awesome Orcas table building Technobloks and letting Alistair do half of my work.

I've decided that as of today, Chauncey Morbyd is no longer my friend. For today, he is officially my enemy.

·16·

A SECRET COMMUNICATION

Dear Alistair,

Can you please write down the secret you were

going to tell me, and then pass the note to me? I

will tear it up after I read it and not show anyone;

I promise.

PLEASE TELL ME!!!

Daniel

P.S. Don't let Chauncey or Mr. Binns see this note!!

P.P.S. Want to build robots after school?

I folded the note into a paper airplane. Then, when Mr. Binns's back was turned and Chauncey had left the table to sharpen his pencil, I flew the airplane note to Alistair. It hit its target perfectly, landing right in front of him.

Unfortunately, Alistair was clueless. He just pushed the airplane away and kept working on what looked like a very complicated math equation that wasn't even on the worksheet.

"Psst—Alistair!" I stood up and pointed toward the paper airplane note sitting next to him. "You're supposed to READ that!"

"Back to work, Daniel!" Mr. Binns pointed to my chair.

I sat back down at my table, but I snuck a peek at Alistair. Luckily, he had finally figured out what I meant. He carefully unfolded my airplane note.

Alistair read my note, then glanced over at me and nodded. Then he started writing his reply.

Every time I snuck a peek at the Orcas work group, I saw Alistair still writing. He wrote for a very, very long time.

That must be one complicated secret, I thought.

· 17 ·

ALISTAIR'S SECRET

Dear Daniel:

Before you read this, you must promise that you will never share my secret with anyone.

Promise?

Okay, good. Here goes:

My family and I tell everyone that we're from Ohio, but that isn't the truth. We are actually from Planet Blaron. We have disguised ourselves as humans and moved to your neighborhood for one important reason: because we have located here the perfect conditions for growing broccoli. (On Planet Blaron, we call it "frackenpoy.")

As you already know, broccoli is virtually the only food we Blaronites can eat. This is a big problem for us. Sadly, our own planet experienced an environmental disaster that wiped out almost every living species and ruined the entire planet's soil. We were no longer able to grow and harvest our beloved frackenpoy naturally.

Luckily, Blaronite scientists developed special farm labs that have prevented starvation. But we cannot produce enough food in labs. We had to venture to distant galaxies in search of a solution.

Our mission here on Earth is to develop and grow new types of broccoli that will survive on Planet Blaron, and send them back to the home planet. We are also here to study the Earth's diverse plant, animal, and insect life. We hope that by studying Earth, we will find ways to make Planet Blaron a healthy place for growing frackenpoy once again.

We are here in peace, but we must conduct our mission in total and complete secrecy until the day when humans are ready to accept our presence. If people discover aliens living in their neighborhood, they may become very frightened and even violent. My parents and I could be captured, locked up in some secret government laboratory, and possibly killed.

You can see how important it is that everything I'm telling you remains top secret.

Daniel, I wish this was the only secret I had to tell you, but there is also something else—something that involves your little brother, Iggy.

Okay, here goes:

You need to know that the material Iggy ingested yesterday may have changed the structure of his DNA.

Why? Because one of the containers contained a Blaronite virus that was created to deliver DNA into an organism. In other words, it's a virus that causes mutations. I was using it to create a new species of broccoli, and I never expected that a human would eat it on purpose.

"Live and learn," as the human saying goes.

In other words, if Iggy consumed the alien virus along with the insect DNA, his human DNA may have already mutated. And based on what we observed this morning, it seems clear that something about Iggy has changed.

Because my mission requires that I attempt to fix any problems I cause on Earth, my colleagues and I attempted to examine Iggy in his sleep last night. Unfortunately, he was very fidgety and our findings were inconclusive. However, I have just heard some good news from our Blaronite medical experts. If we can transport Iggy onto the Spaceship Bumblepod after school today, they will do their best to fix any problems caused by the bug DNA Iggy consumed!

Let's meet at your house after school today, okay? My Blaronite colleagues will transport us onto the Spaceship Bumblepod, and our medical staff will tend to Iggy. You will see that we are "normal people" just like you, and that we Blaronites mean no harm.

Alistair

P.S. And yes—let's build robots later.

·18·

VANISHED!

I **READ ALISTAIR'S LETTER** twice, trying to figure out exactly what it meant.

The letter said that Iggy's DNA may have "mutated." Was Iggy turning into some kind of weird creature? Did an alien virus cause Iggy to pull a car door off its hinges? I had a queasy feeling in my stomach as I remembered my nightmare about Iggy turning into a monster and lifting me toward his giant teeth.

I looked over at Alistair, and he looked

like a completely normal kid. Was Alistair *really* an alien—or was this a big joke? Once again, I felt confused—torn between thinking Alistair was a genius and wondering whether he might be a little crazy.

IS ALISTAIR JUST A WEIRD KID?	IS ALISTAIR AN ALIEN???
Broccoli diet (allergies?)	Broccoli diet (alien digestion?)
Plays with Iggy & Dottie (?)	Plays with Iggy & Dottie (research?)
Collects bugs (hobby)	Combines bugs with alien virus, causing superhuman strength in little brother
Builds models & Gadgets (hobby)	Alien technology makes things fly (the watch)

There was definitely evidence supporting Alistair's story. On the other hand, it was just so hard to believe.

Suddenly, a hand reached in front of me. Before I knew it, the hand snatched both Alistair's secret note and my "weird kid vs. alien" list.

"Whatcha got here, Dano?!" Once again, Chauncey had managed to sneak up behind me.

I tried to grab the letter back, but I wasn't fast enough. Chauncey waved Alistair's secret letter in the air.

"A secret!" he said loudly. "How very interesting!"

I kept trying to tear the letter from his hand, but Chauncey has very long, apelike arms and he kept switching the note from hand to hand.

So much for Alistair's big secret, I thought.

But then something amazing happened: Alistair's note self-destructed right in Chauncey's hand. I'm completely serious: The letter simply *vanished* into thin air! There was a *POP!*, and the next thing I knew, Chauncey held nothing in his hand except a little mound of white dust that looked like a bit of flour or sawdust.

"Ow!" Chauncey yelled. "Hey!"

I stared and stared at Chauncey's empty hand. Where had the letter and my note gone? Did Alistair make that happen? And if so, how?!

"Mr. Binns?" Chauncey yelled. "Daniel brought some kind of *inappropriate* exploding-paper-magic-trick thingy into the classroom, and it burned my hand!"

"Sit down, Chauncey." Mr. Binns sighed. He was used to Chauncey tattling that someone had injured him on purpose.

"But I'm serious, Mr. Binns!" Chauncey insisted.

I caught Alistair's eye and mouthed a silent question: *HOW?*

Alistair pointed to his special watch—*the "magic" watch.*

Wow, I thought. *So Alistair's watch can do more than make objects fly. It can make things disappear. No wonder he didn't want people to use it!*

And then I realized that I believed Alistair's story. *After all,* I thought, *I don't know any human kids who could make a note self-destruct at the exact moment when the wrong person tries to read it!*

I gave Alistair a thumbs-up signal and Alistair smiled.

Chauncey noticed and narrowed his eyes, scowling at us.

So Alistair really is an alien! I thought. I had to admit it was pretty exciting to think that I was friends with a real alien—an alien who trusted nobody with his secret identity!

But then I thought of Iggy and his possibly mutated DNA from an alien virus. I thought of Iggy tearing the door off our van. And suddenly I felt a whole lot more worried than excited.

· 19 ·

ALIEN TECHNOLOGY

"WHY DO THEY call the Blaronite spaceship 'Spaceship Bumblepod'?" I asked.

Alistair and I sat on my front porch, waiting for my mom to come home with Iggy and Dottie. I didn't want to offend Alistair, but I thought the name Spaceship Bumblepod sounded like something that might crash into asteroids or go on really dumb missions.

"I'm not sure *how* it got the name," said Alistair, "but it's home away from home for a lot of Blaronites when they're on missions in search of frackenpoy."

Alistair lifted open one of the little screens on his watch and revealed what looked like hundreds of tiny, glowing bubbles that moved around in different directions.

"What are *those*?" I asked.

"That's the Blaronite language," he explained.

"The Blaronite language is made of *bubbles*?"

"A lot of our technology is bubble powered," he explained, "and this part of the watch is for communications between Earth and Spaceship Bumblepod."

Alistair observed the little floating bubbles that were zipping around, forming different shapes and patterns. "They say that as soon as Iggy gets here, the three of us should get into a single container together so they can transport us up to Spaceship Bumblepod." Alistair snapped the face of his watch shut. "That Gobblebox you showed me in your parents' room would work."

I looked at the complicated buttons and screens on Alistair's watch. "So—what else can you do with that watch?"

Alistair hesitated. "You're asking about classified information."

"But I've *already seen* how you can turn Technoblok models into flying robots and how you make a piece of paper disappear into thin air with that watch. Come on; I promise I'll keep it a secret."

"Okay," said Alistair, "this watch is the most valuable thing I own. It's a communications system, a transport device, an instant-robot generator, and a weapons system for emergencies. It can energize and activate inanimate objects. It can incinerate things or send them into other dimensions or to distant galaxies."

"That's *all*?" I was kidding, but Alistair obviously didn't think my joke was funny. He frowned and pointed the watch at my bicycle, which happened to be leaning against the front porch. As Alistair pushed a button on his watch, my bike's handlebars and pedals turned into spinning propellers.

I jumped to my feet and watched my bike rise up into the sky like a small helicopter. It circled the chimney of my house before landing on the roof.

"Cool! Hey, Alistair! Make the bike fly back down here for a second so I can climb on it for a ride!" I thought it would be pretty fun to fly on a helicopter-bike over my neighborhood.

Alistair pressed another button on his watch and the bike lifted itself from the roof, hovered in the air for a moment, and then gently settled on the ground in front of us.

I jumped onto my bike, but Alistair had apparently changed his mind about letting me fly on it.

"No," he said. "We shouldn't play around with this watch anymore. It's too dangerous."

"Just one quick ride?" I begged. "Please?"

"Someone might see, and then they'd try to steal the watch," said Alistair. "It would be terrible for *everyone* if this watch ever fell into the *wrong hands*."

"Why?" I asked. "I mean, I realize you don't want anyone to know that you're an alien, but—"

"Trust me," said Alistair, looking very upset. "If the wrong person took this watch, it would be the very WORST thing that could happen!"

· 20 ·

INTERSTELLAR VOYAGE

BEFORE I COULD ASK Alistair more questions, my mom pulled up in front of the house. Iggy and Dottie burst from the van and ran to greet me and Alistair: "DANOOOO!! AWISTAIR!!!!"

Iggy suddenly stopped in his tracks. He looked up at the large maple tree in our front yard and jumped amazingly high, grabbing a leafy twig. When he landed he began to chew on the bark.

"Hmmm," said Alistair, observing Iggy.

"We'd better transport him to the Bumblepod as quickly as possible so they can take a look at him."

My mom turned from opening the front door and spied Iggy chewing on tree bark. "Iggy, get that branch out of your mouth!" she said. "Honestly, I don't know what's come over you today. . . . After you have a normal snack you can go back outside and help Dad and me rake the yard if you want to do something with leaves."

"Hello, Iggy!" Alistair grabbed Iggy's arm as Iggy walked into the house. "Come with me and Daniel. We have something really interesting to show you upstairs!"

Iggy nodded. "OKAY, AWISTAIR!"

"Shhhh. We have to be quiet because it's a secret."

Iggy put his finger over his lips. "I be quiet."

While Dottie and my mom went into the kitchen, Iggy, Alistair, and I snuck upstairs to the Gobblebox in my mom's closet. My heart pounded: I could hardly believe that in a matter of minutes I might actually be in outer space, *aboard an alien spacecraft.*

"Where we going, Dano?" Iggy whispered.

"We're playing a fun game called Spaceship Bumblepod," I told him. "First we sneak into Mom and Dad's room and climb into the Gobblebox."

"DA GOBBO-BOX? Oh, AWESOME!"

"Next, we get to visit a real spaceship!"

"OH, DAT SO 'MAZING!!"

"Sh!" I hissed. "If Mom finds us sneaking up here, we'll be in trouble!"

We tiptoed into my parents' room, then made our way toward my mom's closet.

"Now we open da BERFDAY presents, right, Dano?"

"No, Iggy, we're not sneaking birthday presents. We're playing a *new* game called Spaceship Bumblepod, remember?"

"Oh boy!" Iggy clapped his hands.

But when I pushed open my mom's closet door, Iggy froze and shook his head. "Scary!" he whimpered.

"Iggy, that's just the box where Mom and Dad hid our toys," I explained.

Iggy stamped his foot. "I NOT going touch it."

STOMP, STOMP, STOMP. . . . We heard my dad trudging upstairs.

"Quick!" Alistair whispered. "Climb in the box!"

Alistair and I jumped into the Gobblebox, but Iggy hesitated.

"Come on, Iggy!" I whispered, "We'll get in big trouble if Dad finds us up here!"

Iggy finally climbed into the box and stepped on my hand.

"Ow!" I hissed.

"Sowwee, Dano."

We crouched down on top of a pile of plastic models. It wasn't very comfortable in there, but I was still really happy to see my Vortex Chariot again, even though it was broken.

"Iggy?" Dad called. "Are you up here? I'm going outside to rake leaves now!"

"Sh!" I whispered.

"They're not upstairs," I heard my dad call to my mom as he walked back down the steps. "I think they went back outside to play. . . ."

Alistair lifted the communications screen on his watch. I saw those tiny, glowing bubbles racing around, and I suddenly felt very nervous about this whole "space transport" idea. I mean, what if the three of us ended up all mixed up, with our feet where our hands should be—or our brains switched into one another's bodies? I had seen stuff like that happen in cartoons about space travel, and maybe it was possible in real life, too. Besides, Alistair didn't exactly have a good safety track record so far. I mean, if he hadn't left his alien bug-catching equipment in a little kid's room, we wouldn't even *need* to transport Iggy onto the Spaceship Bumblepod.

"Alistair," I said, "are you sure this is safe?"

"Don't worry," said Alistair. "Interstellar transport accidents are only about one in a million these days."

"But what if that one-in-a-million accident happens to *us*?"

Alistair didn't answer; he just pressed a secret button on the transport screen of his watch.

"Hey! What dat AWESOME watch doos?" Iggy reached for Alistair's watch, but something very strange happened before he could grab it.

My heart froze as a beam of light surrounded Iggy.

"What dat light?" Iggy asked.

Iggy vanished. And before I could say a word, the same beam of light surrounded my body, and then Alistair's. At first, I felt tingly and itchy, as if tiny insects were crawling under my skin. Then I felt as if I were floating; I could actually feel myself disappearing.

A moment later, I was gone.

SPACESHIP BUMBLEPOD

I WAS VERY SURPRISED WHEN Iggy, Alistair, and I found ourselves sitting at a table across from my mom and dad. There was a weird assortment of food in front of us. We each had a cup of coffee, a can of whipped cream, and a bag of Goldfish crackers.

Where are we? I wondered, feeling kind of dizzy. What just happened?!

"Look, Dano!" Iggy shouted. "WE GET COF-FEE! And GOLDFISH AND WHIP CREAM!

Dat so YUMMY, right, Dano?" Iggy picked up the can of whipped cream and shook it. It was weird how climbing into a cardboard box and then suddenly finding himself in a completely different world didn't seem to bother Iggy at all.

The room looked like a strange combination of our living room at home, a science lab, and a public bathroom. On one wall, I saw a row of shiny white toilets. Around the room was a drinking fountain, an assortment of machine parts and gadgets, and a gumball machine. On another wall, I saw some closed doors labeled with weird signs: UNDERPANTS, CONTROL, SUPERHERO COSTUMES, PRINCESS ROOM.

What kind of crazy spaceship was this? I wondered. Why were my mom and dad here? And why were they just sitting there, staring at us?!

"My colleagues on Spaceship Bumblepod scanned Iggy's mind in advance in order to

disguise themselves as familiar humans," Alistair explained. "They didn't want him to feel too scared by an alien environment."

No wonder everything is so strange here, I thought. It's like being inside Iggy's nutball head. I suddenly realized that the Blaronites' ability to scan human minds must be the reason Alistair resembled Zip Starwagon. Had he and his parents "scanned my mind" in order to pick a disguise that would appeal to me? And was that why Alistair owned so many amazing Planet Blaster models? The idea freaked me out a little, to be honest.

"Do you like the snacks we chose for you?" the alien mom asked.

"We picked some of your favorites," said the alien dad.

"Well, more Iggy's favorites," said the alien mom.

"That's true," said the alien dad. "More Iggy's favorites."

It figures, I thought. Iggy probably would pick whipped cream and coffee for a snack if he could get away with it.

"My name is Miss Bubble," said the alien who looked like my mom.

"Your name is Mommy!" said Iggy, pointing at her.

"You can call me 'Mommy' if you want," said Miss Bubble.

"And my name is Mr. Stickyfoot," said the other alien, who looked like my dad. "Welcome to the Spaceship Bumblepod—our home away from home."

"Miss Bubble and Mr. Stickyfoot are Chief Medical Experts on Spaceship Bumblepod," Alistair explained.

"Nice to meet you," I said.

"And you as well, Daniel," said Mr. Stickyfoot. "Once we've examined your little brother and performed a couple tests, you'll have a chance to visit Planet Blaron—our home planet—so you can learn a little more about us."

Iggy eyed the alien mom and dad across the table, probably wondering why they weren't grabbing the whipped cream away from him.

I knew what Iggy was thinking: This might be the perfect opportunity to just *go for it*—the long-awaited whipped-cream-mountain experiment.

It's funny that Iggy doesn't even realize he's on an alien spaceship, I thought. *All he can think about is that can of whipped cream.*

"Now, Iggy," said Miss Bubble, "while you shake that can of whipped cream, we're going to take a look at you, okay?"

Iggy nodded.

"Iggy," said Miss Bubble, "Alistair tells us you put something yucky in your mouth yesterday."

"I eat bugs!" Iggy announced.

"I see," said Miss Bubble. "What kinds?"

"Big ones, creepy and crawly ones, and yucky, ooey-gooey ones. And a ladybug. And bug candy!"

As Iggy spoke, Mr. Stickyfoot looked inside Iggy's ears and nose.

Next, Miss Bubble and Mr. Stickyfoot reached into their pockets and pulled out fluffy objects that looked like giant feather dusters.

"What dose fluff balls doos?" Iggy asked.

Instead of answering, Mr. Stickyfoot and Miss Bubble lifted Iggy's shirt and proceeded to tickle him all over.

Iggy squirmed and giggled like crazy.

"What kind of medical test is *that*?" I asked Alistair. Were Mr. Stickyfoot and Miss Bubble real "medical experts"—or was this just a game based on some silly idea in Iggy's mind?

"Those tickle sticks are actually our most advanced medical evaluation tools," Alistair explained.

If this is what it's like going to the doctor on Planet Blaron, I thought, *I guess the aliens have it a lot better than we do on Earth!* I mean, I'd take one of those "tickle sticks" over a flu shot any day.

By the time Mr. Stickyfoot and Miss Bubble finished tickling Iggy, he lay on the ground, gasping for breath, but still laughing.

Mr. Stickyfoot and Miss Bubble opened a metal box that looked like a small freezer and stuck the tickle sticks inside.

"In a few minutes, we'll have a complete DNA report. Then we'll take a look at the data and make our recommendations," said Mr. Stickyfoot.

"Should we send the boys to Planet Blaron orientation while we wait?" Miss Bubble asked.

"Planet Blaron orientation?!" The word "orientation" always makes me nervous because it reminds me of the first day of school.

"I think they're ready," said Mr. Stickyfoot. "Alistair, you stay here so we can discuss our findings with you first. Boys—prepare yourselves to visit Planet Blaron!"

A ray of light surrounded Iggy and me.

"AWESOME!" Just before we disappeared, Iggy managed to blast Miss Bubble and Mr. Stickyfoot with a mountain of whipped cream.

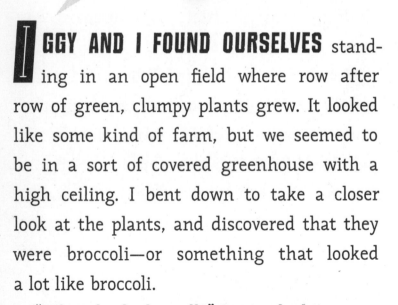

· 22 ·

PLANET BLARON

IGGY AND I FOUND OURSELVES standing in an open field where row after row of green, clumpy plants grew. It looked like some kind of farm, but we seemed to be in a sort of covered greenhouse with a high ceiling. I bent down to take a closer look at the plants, and discovered that they were broccoli—or something that looked a lot like broccoli.

"What dat bad smell?" Iggy asked.

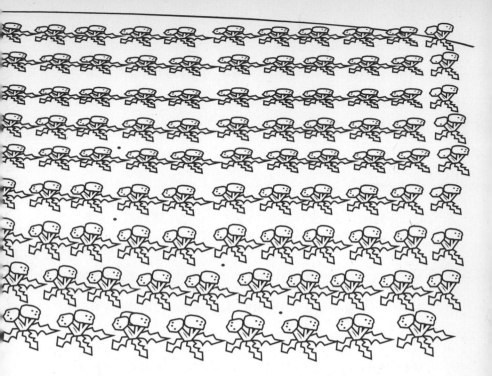

He was right; the air stunk like a pile of dirty socks. On the other hand, I supposed it was lucky that we could breathe at all, since we were on an alien planet.

"What dis place called, Dano?"

"I guess we're on Planet Blaron." I wondered if someone was going to show up and explain what, exactly, we were doing on this alien broccoli farm.

"Why Planet Blaron?" Iggy looked scared,

and I wondered how much longer he would put up with this so-called "game" of traveling to Planet Blaron.

"Remember, Iggy," I said, "we're just pretending."

"Pretend like a movie?" Iggy asked.

"Yes—like a movie." I figured there was no reason to scare Iggy more than necessary, since there was no telling what he might do if he *really* freaked out. I secretly felt terrified, wondering what Alistair, Mr. Stickyfoot, and Miss Bubbles might do to us next. What if Iggy and I got stranded here on Planet Blaron with nothing to eat but raw broccoli?

Something moved overhead, and when I looked up, I realized that what I thought was a gray ceiling above us was actually *alive*. Whatever it was looked squishy, gray, and snaky. It made me think of a giant, writhing brain. Staring up at it, I felt queasy.

Then I thought I might faint when some-

thing that resembled a living hot-air balloon dropped down from the sky.

"LOOK, DANO!" Iggy shouted. "BALLOON!!"

The balloon creature drifted slowly through the air with tentacles dangling. Part of its body seemed to be a baggy sac that functioned like a parachute.

As it moved closer to us, I saw that the creature had three large eyeballs attached to long stalks on its head. It was enormous.

Part of me wanted to scream and run away,

but Iggy was watching me to see whether he should be worried. I knew I should try to act brave.

"What dat name dat animo called, Dano?" Iggy asked. "Dat squid or giant space octopus or balloon-eyeball monster?"

"I'm not sure, Iggy," I croaked. Iggy was looking to me for all the answers, but I didn't have any.

We watched the alien squid creature settle near a large clump of broccoli and release something that reminded me of a giant suction cup or an enormous snail's foot from inside its body. The giant foot-stomach covered the broccoli plant and devoured it.

At least that alien seems to be more interested in the broccoli than in us, I thought.

I remembered how the aliens had made themselves look like our mom and dad "to make us feel more comfortable." *I guess this is how the Blaronites really look,* I thought. To be honest, this didn't make my stomach feel any better.

"UP! UP!" Suddenly, Iggy was screaming. "PICK ME UP, DANO! I SCARED!"

I looked up and saw more aliens dropping from the high ceiling like a team of skydivers. A moment, later, we were surrounded by several of the baggy, slimy creatures.

Iggy screamed as loud as he could: "I WANNA GO HOOOOOME!!"

· 23 ·

A MOSTLY NORMAL BOY

THE MOMENT IGGY SCREAMED, our environment changed. We instantly found ourselves back on the Spaceship Bumblepod, seated across from Alistair, Miss Bubble, and Mr. Stickyfoot.

Iggy threw himself on Alistair in a bear hug. "Awistair—we saw giant space octopus! And it have a very gwoss booger-glue slime-bag dat come out of his tummy and cover dat plant and a big balloon-head thing wif three

GINORMOUS EYEBALLS, and it was a BIG, YUCK-O MONSTER!"

Miss Bubble and Mr. Stickyfoot said nothing. I got the feeling Iggy might have hurt their feelings by using words like "gwoss" and "yuck-o" and "slime-bag" to describe the Blaronite creatures.

"That creature wasn't a monster, Iggy," said Alistair.

"But it look very YUCKY!" said Iggy.

I glanced at Alistair and tried to imagine what he might look like without his human disguise. It kind of bothered me. Those aliens were just so *weird looking*.

But who knows, maybe we humans looked kind of gross to Alistair, too.

"Shall we get started?" said Mr. Stickyfoot, who sounded a little impatient. "We've finished our analysis of Iggy's DNA, and we're ready to share the results."

"Here, Iggy," said Alistair, opening one of

the panels on his watch. "Why don't you take a look at one of your favorite cartoons for a few minutes while Daniel and I talk to Mr. Stickyfoot and Miss Bubbles?" At the push of a button, a *Spongebob* episode appeared on Alistair's watch.

"AWESOME!" Iggy couldn't believe his luck. A huge grin spread across Iggy's face as Alistair put the special Blaronite watch on his wrist.

"You're letting Iggy wear your watch?" I couldn't believe it, after all of Alistair's talk about the dangers of the alien watch "falling into the wrong hands."

"Don't worry," Alistair whispered, "the watch is automatically under the Bumble-pod's control while we're on board the space-ship. It's on SAFE mode right now, so its powers are deactivated until we leave the ship."

I secretly wished Alistair had put the

watch on my wrist instead of Iggy's because I also love *Spongebob*. But I guess I was stuck talking to the aliens about Iggy's DNA problem while Iggy sat and giggled, watching his cartoon.

"Daniel," said Mr. Stickyfoot, "the good news is that Iggy is still *mostly* a normal human boy."

"What do you mean, '*mostly*' normal?" I asked.

"We mean that most of his DNA is still human," said Miss Bubbles.

"And what about the rest of his DNA?" I asked.

"Well, some *insect and arachnid genes* are now part of Iggy's genetic code."

I stared at the three of them. "You're telling me that Iggy is part insect and spider now?"

"Exactly," said Mr. Stickyfoot.

"Iggy is turning into a BUG?!" I exclaimed.

"Well, he's not exactly going to *turn into* a bug," said Alistair, "but as Iggy grows, he may have a few *bug traits*. Or more specifically, a few insect and spider traits."

"What sort of 'insect and spider traits'?!"

"That is unpredictable," said Mr. Stickyfoot.

"But I need to know!" I insisted. "I have to share a room with Iggy, and I'd kind of like a warning if he's suddenly going to wake up with an antenna on his head, or start flying around the room, or grow a stinger on his butt!"

"Ooooooooo, Dano say a bad word!" Iggy yelled from across the room.

"I fail to see a disadvantage in any of those scenarios," said Mr. Stickyfoot.

"Here, Daniel, let me show you a picture that might help you understand what we're looking at." Miss Bubble touched the table in front of us, and it turned into a computer screen. Suddenly a complicated pattern appeared.

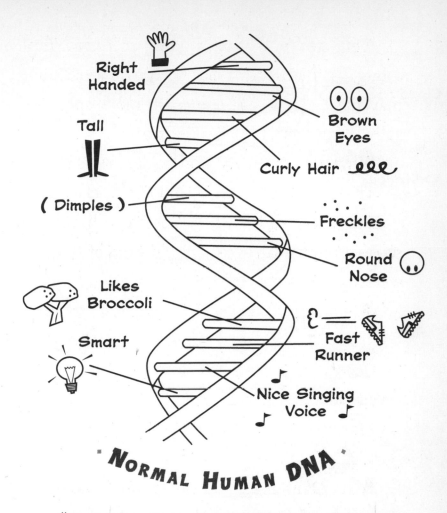

Right Handed

Tall

(Dimples)

Likes Broccoli

Smart

Brown Eyes

Curly Hair

Freckles

Round Nose

Fast Runner

Nice Singing Voice

NORMAL HUMAN DNA

"See? This is a picture of normal human DNA: It's kind of like the secret code inside each of your cells that determines all your human traits. Now—take a look at a picture of Iggy's *mutated* DNA."

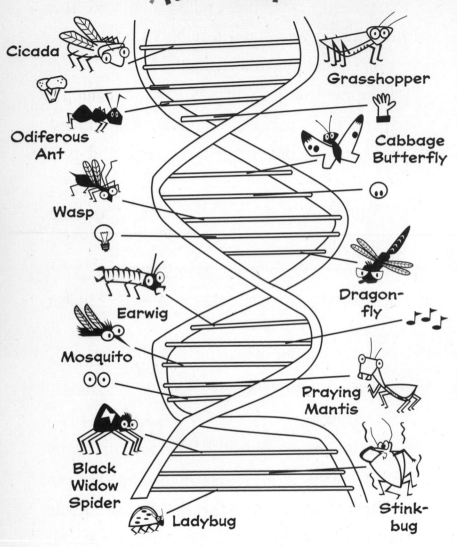

Iggy's DNA

Cicada

Odiferous
Ant

Wasp

Earwig

Mosquito

Black
Widow
Spider

Ladybug

Grasshopper

Cabbage
Butterfly

Dragon-
fly

Praying
Mantis

Stink-
bug

Miss Bubble tapped the table again and a
new picture appeared.

I didn't know what to think. I half expected

to suddenly wake up and realize that this whole thing was just a terrible nightmare.

"So let me get this straight," I said. "You're telling me that Iggy is now part grasshopper, part ladybug, part cicada, part odiferous ant, part cabbage butterfly, part wasp, and part mosquito."

"Among a few other species," said Mr. Stickyfoot. "You forgot stinkbug, for example. There's also some evidence of possible slug DNA, which is, of course, not in the insect category."

"And Iggy will develop some *traits* of those insects—and spiders and slugs or whatever—as he grows up."

"He *might*," said Mr. Stickyfoot, "but only *if he's lucky*."

"Or he might not," said Alistair, who knew that I didn't consider *any* of this the least bit lucky.

"Daniel, keep in mind that just because a creature has a particular gene doesn't always mean that the gene will *express itself*," said Miss Bubbles.

"That's right," said Mr. Stickyfoot. "Iggy might go through his whole life without ever developing a stinger, or wings, or venom. Of course, that would be a pity, in my opinion. Insects are such amazing creatures; from what I read in Alistair's Earth research, I would think any human would be very pleased to have as many insect parts as possible."

"Well, you couldn't be more wrong about *that*," I said. *Especially when that human is your little brother,* I thought.

What could be worse than sharing a room with regular Iggy? I asked myself. *How about sharing a room with poisonous, stinging, insect-Iggy with superhuman strength?!*

"Listen," I said. "You guys are aliens, and your technology is way more advanced than the stuff we have on Earth. Can't you just turn him back into a *normal* human again?"

"The problem with that," said Mr. Sticky-foot, "is that we're not very familiar with 'normal' human DNA. Besides, it's always much easier to mess things up than it is to fix them."

I glared at Alistair. *This is all your fault!* I thought.

"You should also know that Iggy's environment and emotions may affect his development," said Miss Bubbles. "For example, if he gets very angry or frightened, his body will produce chemicals that could activate his insect DNA. If he stays very calm at all times, he's more likely to remain a normal human boy."

I snorted. "Iggy hasn't been calm for a single day of his entire life!"

Alistair looked at Miss Bubbles and Mr. Stickyfoot. "Maybe we should tell Daniel the *good* news now."

"What good news?" I asked.

"They've invented something that will help Iggy return to normal if his insect DNA starts to take over."

Miss Bubbles nodded. "I'll get the Human Normalizer," she said.

"The *Human Normalizer*?"

Miss Bubbles walked over to a control panel and pressed a bunch of buttons. A sliding door opened up, and she returned to the table carrying something that looked like a silver platter you might see at a fancy dinner party, with a dome-shaped lid on top.

"Open it, Daniel," said Miss Bubbles, after placing the platter thing on the table.

I lifted the heavy lid and stared at what lay underneath. "What the—?"

I couldn't believe it.

"A pacifier?! The Human Normalizer is a pacifier?!"

"But it's not just a *regular* pacifier," said Alistair. "It's made with the most advanced Blaronite technology."

"That's right," said Miss Bubbles. "If a stressful event triggers Iggy's insect mutations, just give him this as soon as possible. In most cases, it should help him return to normal."

"In theory, at least," said Mr. Stickyfoot.

I sensed that Alistair, Mr. Stickyfoot, and Miss Bubbles actually had no idea whether the Human Normalizer pacifier would work. But since I had no other options at the moment, I stuck the alien pacifier in my pocket to take home.

"Is there any other way we can be of help before you leave, Daniel?" Miss Bubbles asked.

I felt like saying something very rude, but I stopped myself. "Well," I said, "could you also create some Bug-Boy Insect Repellent Spray for me to use when Iggy starts bugging me?"

Alistair let out a giggle. "That was a joke, right? Good one!"

"No, Alistair," I said. "That was NOT a joke."

Because it wasn't.

ROBOTS AND LADYBUGS

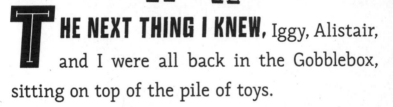

THE NEXT THING I KNEW, Iggy, Alistair, and I were all back in the Gobblebox, sitting on top of the pile of toys.

"Iggy!" It was Dottie, calling from downstairs. "Where you go?"

Without waiting a moment, Iggy sprang out of the Gobblebox and raced down the steps. "Dottie! I go in da Gobbo-box and see a SPACE-OCTOPUS SQUID THINGY AND ALSO SPONGEBOB ON A WATCH!"

It amazed me that Iggy had so much energy after traveling to Spaceship Bumblepod, Planet Blaron, and back to Earth. I still felt dizzy from being transported all over the place.

"You might need to drink some water," Alistair said. "Space transport can be very dehydrating."

I started scooping up Technobloks from the Gobblebox and hiding them in my pockets. I figured that I deserved to get some of my toys back after going through such a weird experience.

Alistair looked at me with that I'm-reading-your-mind expression he gets. "Um—are we still friends?"

What could I say? To be honest, I was mad at Alistair. *Really* mad. "I didn't sign up for this," I blurted.

"Sign up for what?"

"Having a little brother who might turn into an insect-boy."

"Oh," said Alistair. "Yeah. I know."

The two of us just sat there in the Gobble-box for a minute, not saying anything.

Alistair noticed a ladybug crawling along the windowsill, so he grabbed it and cupped it in his hand. "These are my favorite Earth bugs," said Alistair. "Although they're actually beetles, not bugs."

"Bugs, bugs, bugs," I said, still feeling annoyed. "What's so great about bugs?"

"One reason they're my favorite is because they eat pests that can ruin your broccoli crop. And for another thing, they squirt green blood from their knees when they're in danger."

"Really?" That was pretty weird. "I didn't know that."

Alistair blew on the ladybug and it flew away.

"You know," said Alistair, "when my family first moved here, I hated everything about being on Earth."

"So?"

Neither of us said anything for a minute. I looked at Alistair and tried to imagine what it must feel like for him. How would I feel if *my* parents told me that I had to move to a different planet where I had no friends, and where I had to wear a disguise every day? I guessed it would be pretty hard. I knew Alistair must be amazingly brave.

I also knew it was sort of also my fault that Iggy had eaten the bug DNA. After all, I had snuck up to the Gobblebox right when I was supposed to watch him.

But I was still mad at Alistair.

"I used to hate being here," Alistair continued, "but then I realized that there are all kinds of cool things to study on Earth—like insects and plants, and that there are *way* more species here than on Planet Blaron. And of course, I'm helping everyone back on the home planet by finding better ways to grow frackenpoy."

Alistair looked at me. "Remember when you and Chauncey were at my house and I couldn't stop laughing?"

"Yeah," I said, remembering how Alistair had rolled around, giggling about nothing for about an hour while I sat and played with his Technobloks. "So what was your deal?"

"Well, I can't explain why I started laughing, but I had never laughed before in my whole life."

"Never?"

"Blaronites don't laugh," he said. "Anyway, once I started, I just couldn't stop. And that was the first moment I realized it could actually be *fun* to be human. And now that we're friends, I don't think about wanting to go back to Planet Blaron so much. I want to live here."

I wasn't sure what to say. I had to admit that things had gotten a lot more exciting since Alistair had moved in next door. On the other hand, I now had a bunch of new problems.

Alistair picked up the Vortex Chariot and looked at it. "Now this one would make a cool robot," he said. "Don't you think?"

Hearing that cheered me up a little. "You know what would be even *cooler* robot?" I said. "The Sargonian Desolator."

"But the Vortex Chariot has better weapons."

"You DARE to challenge the Sargonian Desolator?!" I grabbed the Vortex Chariot and hid it under my shirt as I climbed out of the Gobblebox.

"Okay," said Alistair, "maybe I do."

I handed Alistair some extra Technobloks and we tiptoed downstairs and into my room. I was still kind of mad, but not so mad that I didn't want to build robots.

· 25 ·

FRIENDS AND ENEMIES

"I HAVE A GREAT IDEA," said Alistair. "Let's build a *Brocco-bot!*"

"What's a Brocco-bot?"

"A robot that will help grow the perfect broccoli plant."

"Okay, Alistair," I said, blocking the doorway to my room, "that's where I draw the line. We are NOT building a Brocco-bot!"

"But it would be so useful!"

"Exactly. It would be so lame and totally NOT cool!"

Just then, the doorbell rang, and I heard Iggy race from the kitchen to open it. "CHAAAAAUNCEEEE!"

Uh-oh, I thought. *Just the person I don't want to see right now.*

"It smells like cookies in here!" Chauncey announced. But instead of looking for a snack like he usually does, Chauncey walked straight toward my room. "Hey, Daniel! Can you show me how you did that fake exploding letter-magic-trick thing—"

Chauncey froze when he saw Alistair. "Oh," he said, in a not-friendly voice. "I didn't realize Broccoli Boy was here."

"Hi, Chauncey," said Alistair. He didn't seem to notice Chauncey's mean attitude and just kept working on his Brocco-bot.

"So, Daniel," said Chauncey, "How about showing me that magic-trick thing you did at school?"

"What magic trick?" I knew I had to play dumb. There was no way a tattletale like

Chauncey could be trusted with a secret as huge as aliens living next door, not to mention a watch that transports people into outer space.

"You know," said Chauncey, "that letter I picked up at school. The paper that just disappeared in my hand!"

"Maybe you shouldn't pick up letters that don't belong to you."

"Whatever," said Chauncey. "Just show me how you did it, okay?"

"Look, Chauncey, there isn't any trick."

Chauncey squinted at Alistair. "What about you, Broccoli Boy? I bet you also know how it works!"

Alistair just shrugged and kept building with Technobloks.

"Fine," said Chauncey. "Be that way."

"Chauncey! Come quick!" Iggy ran up to Chauncey and tugged on his sleeve. "I find one bwoken animo cwacker and five marsho-wowows on da floor!"

I was relieved when Chauncey followed Iggy to the kitchen to check out the "marsho-wowows." *With any luck, they'll keep playing together until dinnertime,* I thought.

"Okay, Alistair," I said. "So how do we build this Brocco-bot?" I still wasn't too excited about Alistair's Brocco-bot idea, but I figured it was better than getting dragged into

a game of Squidboy versus the Blue Freaks with Chauncey and Iggy. I especially wanted to avoid Chauncey because his suspicious questions about the disappearing paper made me nervous. What if Chauncey figured out the truth—that Alistair is actually an alien? I realized Iggy might blab something about getting transported to Planet Blaron, but since Iggy often talks about all kinds of imaginary things, I figured Chauncey wouldn't pay much attention to him.

· 26 ·

DO NOT TOUCH THIS BUTTON!

ALISTAIR WAS JUST SHOWING ME how to install a tiny motor in our Brocco-bot when we heard loud crashing and shouting noises coming from upstairs. It sounded like Iggy and Chauncey were playing a game of Squidboy that was getting out of control. I kept expecting to hear my mom or dad run upstairs and tell them to stop, but no grown-ups seemed to be around.

Then I noticed something that worried me: "Hey, Alistair," I said, "where's your watch?"

Alistair's face turned pale when he looked down at his wrist and realized that his watch was gone. "Oh no. . . . I never got it back from Iggy after he borrowed it to watch cartoons on Spaceship Bumblepod!" Alistair jumped to his feet and ran from the room.

"See?" I called, following Alistair up the stairs. "I knew it was a bad idea to let Iggy borrow that watch!"

Upstairs, we found Iggy and Chauncey fighting over Alistair's watch, which (luckily!) was still on Iggy's wrist.

Just let me see that watch for a second!

NO! DIS WATCH MINES!!

I knew I should try to separate the two of them right away, but I hesitated because it was actually kind of funny to see Iggy pinning Chauncey to the ground. I hesitated for a moment, just watching them.

Alistair was just relieved that Iggy hadn't accidentally used the watch to send himself to some distant planet.

"Um, excuse me, Iggy," said Alistair, "could I please have my watch back?"

"NEVER!" said Iggy. "Dis watch MINES!"

Alistair just stared at Iggy. "That doesn't even make sense."

"Welcome to the world of little brothers, Alistair." I fixed Iggy with my most serious big-brother stare. "Iggy," I said, "you KNOW that watch does NOT belong to you, so give it back RIGHT NOW."

Iggy burst into tears. "IT MINES! Awistair say I can HAVE it!"

"I said you could *borrow* it," Alistair explained.

"Big mistake," I muttered.

Iggy sobbed. As he wiped his nose with his sleeve, I noticed that he relaxed his grip on Chauncey for a moment. I decided we should seize the opportunity to get Alistair's watch back: *"Now!"* I whispered to Alistair. *"I'll hold him; you grab the watch!"*

Alistair and I made a dive for Iggy and the watch.

Apparently Chauncey had the same idea because he suddenly managed to wriggle out of Iggy's grasp.

Unfortunately for all three of us, Iggy's reflexes were a lot faster than we expected.

And unfortunately for Chauncey, that's when something *really* terrible happened:

"WHOA!" Iggy's eyes grew wide as the Gobblebox shook and jumped around like a creature coming to life.

What was happening to Chauncey in there?

"This is bad." Alistair looked even paler than he did when he first learned that Iggy ate his research insects. "I think Iggy activated the Insta-Monster function on the watch."

"The insta-what?"

"Insta-Monster combines the molecular structures of two or more objects and creates a completely new life-form—a creature that has the *worst* characteristics of each of its components."

I stared at the box, which actually seemed to be alive—almost *breathing*. "You mean," I said—

"Yes," said Alistair. "A Chauncey-Gobblebox monster is forming right in front of us."

A monster with all of Chauncey Morbyd's worst qualities?! "Alistair," I said, "we have to stop it!"

I grabbed Iggy's arms and shook him. "Iggy, give Alistair his watch right now, so Alistair can stop this!"

"NO!" Iggy shouted, pulling away from me and grinning at the jumping Gobblebox. He was obviously enjoying the sound of Chauncey's muffled voice, calling for help from inside the box. "MY WATCH!" Iggy yelled. "MY GOBBO-BOX!"

To Iggy, this is all a big, entertaining game, I thought. I had to admit that I could understand why he didn't want to give back the watch. Why would he give up the watch now that he could make such exciting things happen?

"Iggy," I said, trying to make my voice sound calmer, "you have to listen. If you don't give Alistair the watch, Chauncey is going to turn into a REAL MONSTER."

"What kind of monster he be?"

"I don't *know* what kind! Just give me—"

"It's too late," Alistair yelled. "Duck and cover NOW!"

INSTA-MONSTER

WHEN THE DUST SETTLED, we stared and stared at what used to be the Gobblebox—and what used to be Chauncey. Now, instead of two things, there was one horrible creature— something that should never exist on Earth or any other planet.

The creature was shaped like a giant cube that wore Chauncey's clothes. I could see Chauncey's little features—his beady eyes and small ears and nose on the surface of the cube—but most of the boxy body was a huge, drooling mouth.

From across the room, I could smell the monster's marshmallow-breath. The monster's hair was a clumpy mass of Technobloks; his hands were like robot claws made from bits of Planet Blaster vehicles.

"Yuck," said Iggy, looking at the Chauncey-monster. "No like it."

"Gobbo," said the monster. "Gobbo-gobbo!"

Iggy giggled. "He say, 'gobbo-gobbo'!"

This made the monster angry. The Gobble-box monster stood up and ROARED at Iggy.

We all screamed and dove under my parents' bed to hide. Was this going to be the end of us? I wondered. Were the three of us going to be eaten by Chauncey Morbyd in monster form?

But instead of coming after us, the monster turned and clomped heavily down the stairs yelling "GOBBO-GOBBO-GOBBO!!"

If this monster has Chauncey's worst qualities, I thought, *he'll definitely head for the kitchen to look for a sugary snack.*

We heard a scream from downstairs. It was Dottie.

"I help you, Dottie!" Iggy jumped to his feet and raced downstairs to rescue Dottie from the monster. Alistair and I followed close behind.

But it turned out the monster wasn't interested in Dottie or the dolls she kept throwing at him.

Just as I suspected, the Chauncey-Gobblebox monster stood in the kitchen, tossing anything sweet he could find into his giant mouth.

"Alistair," I whispered, "what are we going to do?"

"I'm not sure," said Alistair. "I've never reversed an insta-monster before."

"Well, this is probably a good time to try!"

By now, the Gobblebox had eaten everything sugary he could find in the refrigerator and he was growing restless. He drank from a carton of milk but threw it on the ground when he realized it wasn't chocolate milk. He opened a Tupperware container to sample a bite of leftover meat lasagna, but tossed it across the room when he realized it wasn't sweet. "GOBBO-GOBBO-GOBBO!!" he yelled.

Dottie kept hitting the monster with her doll. "GO 'WAY YOU STINKY, GWOSS BOX-GUY!"

Iggy just giggled as he watched the Gobblebox monster make a huge mess in the kitchen.

"Iggy," I said, "you have to give Alistair his watch so he can try to free Chauncey from this Gobblebox monster."

"No," said Iggy. "Dis watch mines."

"IGGY, CHAUNCEY HAS TURNED INTO A MONSTER THAT'S EATING THE ENTIRE REFRIGERATOR, AND YOU STILL WON'T GIVE BACK THE WATCH?!"

Iggy just grinned. "Nope!"

That was the last straw. I tackled Iggy and tried to grab the watch.

But I forgot how extremely strong Iggy had grown in the past day. Instead of grabbing the watch from Iggy, I only managed to press another one of the control buttons by accident.

THE
INSTA-GROW
FUNCTION FOR MONSTERS
SUPER SIZE YOUR
INSTA-MONSTER WITH
APPETITE
ACCELERATOR!!

"Oh no," said Alistair. "You hit the insta-grow appetite accelerator!"

"What does that mean?" I asked.

We heard a loud gurgling sound that seemed to come from inside the Gobblebox— or from inside Chauncey.

"What dat noise?" Iggy asked.

"He's hungry," said Alistair.

"We already know that."

"I mean he's *REALLY* hungry."

Alistair wasn't kidding. We stared as the Gobblebox ate the salt-and-pepper shakers and then started on the pots and pans. And when he finished eating the pots and pans, he gobbled up the telephone, my mom's address book, some silverware, a pot holder, and some of Iggy's and Dottie's babyish artwork.

"Stop!" Iggy shouted. "Dat my dwawing!"

"See, Iggy?" I pointed at the Gobblebox, who was now eating our television. "If you don't give Alistair that watch right now, the monster is going to eat ALL OF OUR TOYS!"

"And it will eat your whole house," said Alistair. "And then he'll eat my house, and the whole town. Eventually, he'll eat the planet."

"Alistair, you don't have to exaggerate."

"I'm not exaggerating," said Alistair. "I'm completely serious."

I looked at the Gobblebox monster and saw

that it had grown. It was so tall, its flat head now pressed up against the ceiling.

"The appetite-accelerator button speeds up the monster's growth," Alistair explained. "Everything it eats gives it more energy to consume. This Gobblebox monster will literally *eat the entire universe* if we don't find a way to shut it down in the next few minutes!"

The monster did seem to be eating twice as fast, now putting anything and everything into its mouth. Dottie screamed as it tossed her favorite stuffed animal into its mouth pit.

A tiny drip of common sense must have finally seeped into Iggy's brain, because he reluctantly removed the watch from his wrist. But just as he was handing it over to Alistair, a giant Technoblok hand reached down and snatched the watch away.

Alistair, Iggy, Dottie, and I all watched in horror as the Gobblebox gulped down Alistair's watch.

"Give it back!" I pounded on the monster's flat, cardboard back. "Chauncey Morbyd, I know you're in there somewhere!" I shouted. "You have to give us that watch!"

"He probably can't understand you," Alistair explained. "Remember, the monster most likely has only Chauncey's appetite—not his intelligence."

The monster chuckled. "Heh, heh, gobbo-gobbo, heh!"

Suddenly I felt the cold squeeze of plastic Technoblok fingers around my waist as the monster lifted me toward his dank mouth filled with sharp, plaque-stained teeth.

I closed my eyes and braced for the worst.

· 28 ·

THE SUPERKID

I **SQUEEZED MY EYES SHUT** and braced for the impact of Chauncey's monster teeth. *This is it!* I thought.

Far below, I heard Iggy and Dottie screaming: "NOOOOO! PUT DANO DOWN!!"

But then something completely amazing happened: instead of sharp teeth, something green and lumpy bumped me in the head—a bunch of broccoli!

The monster didn't like broccoli; it coughed

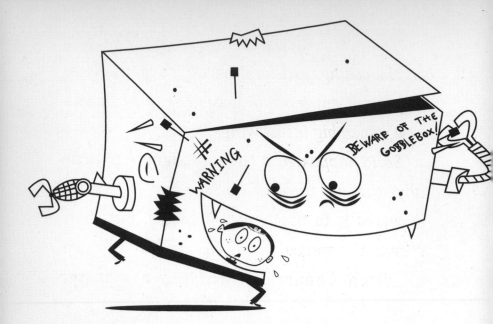

and gagged. Finally, the Gobblebox spit me out onto the floor.

"Hooray!" Dottie shouted and clapped. "Dat monster hate veggies!"

"Good thinking, Dottie!" said Alistair.

But now the Gobblebox was angrier than ever. He punched a wall with a Technoblok fist and cracked the plaster.

"Where's Iggy?" I asked.

Alistair pointed up toward the ceiling. And that's when I saw something unbelievable: *Iggy was perched upside down* on the ceiling, just as if he were a housefly or a spider. Even more amazing: *Iggy had somehow grown big insect wings.*

So it happened, I thought. *Iggy has actually turned into an insect-boy.* I hadn't expected it to happen so suddenly. But then, I hadn't expected to travel to outer space or watch Chauncey turn into a monster either.

"The stress of seeing you being attacked by the Gobblebox monster must have activated Iggy's insect DNA," Alistair explained.

"IGGY!" Dottie had just now spied her brother perched on the ceiling overhead. "HOW YOU GET WINGS?"

"THEY GROWDED ON ME SO I CAN SAVE YOU!" Iggy yelled. "I SAVE YOU FROM DAT MONSTER, DOTTIE! I SAVE YOU, AWISTAIR AND DANO!"

Then Iggy attacked the Gobblebox.

*   *   *

· 29 ·

AN ARMY OF ROBOTS

IT WAS FUNNY HOW, after seeing so many strange things during the past few hours, the sight of my little brother flying around the room like a giant insect seemed almost normal. Well, maybe not *normal*—just not as shocking as you would think. Besides, Iggy really seemed to be enjoying himself.

"Iggy, you a superkid!" said Dottie.

We all cheered for Iggy, who just grinned and flew around the room. He looked very happy to be part insect, at least for the moment.

"Iggy!" Dottie shouted. "Give me a ride!"

Iggy stopped and let Dottie climb on his back for a bug ride through the air. Dottie giggled like crazy as Iggy soared over the wreckage in our kitchen.

Who knows, I thought, *maybe life as an insect-boy might be perfect for Iggy.*

But I didn't have any more time to think about Iggy's future because Alistair and I had some big problems to solve. For one thing, the house looked like about five tornados had blown through it. For another thing, we had a giant, unconscious monster pinned to the ground—a hideous monster that contained Chauncey.

Chauncey's mother would soon be calling him home for dinner. How would we explain what had happened to her son?

"Iggy? Daniel? Dottie? Where are you?"

I heard my mom calling for us; she and my dad were still outside raking the leaves.

"I'll look over at Chauncey's house," I heard

my dad say. "You could check the new kid's house next door."

"Alistair," I said, "my mom and dad are going to come back inside any minute, so there's no way we'll be able to keep them from finding out what happened."

"Maybe," said Alistair, wiping some monster slime from his watch, "but I might have just enough time to fix this." Alistair opened his watch's communications screen and tapped out an emergency message.

I saw the little bubbles inside his watch moving in response to his communication.

"Okay," Alistair said, apparently reading some instructions from Spaceship Bumblepod. "We might be able to get this under control if we get some help."

"We need an *army* of help," I said.

"Exactly," said Alistair. "Quick—go gather a bunch of toys. We'll need as many robots as possible."

Suddenly, I understood Alistair's idea: *his*

watch can generate instant robots to help us fix everything!

I ran to my room and gathered the Broccobot and the vehicles we had managed to sneak out of the Gobblebox earlier. Then I grabbed a bunch of dolls and stuffed animals from Dottie's room and brought everything back to Alistair.

Alistair tapped a series of commands on his watch and the next thing we knew, a team of small robots got busy picking up broken glass, wiping up spilled lasagna, sealing cracked plaster on the wall, and repairing broken furniture. It was awesome, like something out of a fairy tale!

"The house already looks better," I said, watching the robots scurrying around at high speed. "But what about the Chauncey Monster lying here on the floor?"

"My colleagues on the Bumblepod gave me a special code to reverse the chemical reactions that fused Chauncey and the Gobblebox into a monster."

"You mean, Chauncey will go back to being a semi-normal boy again?"

"I'll do my best." Alistair tapped a complicated pattern of controls on his watch. "We're lucky that Iggy managed to subdue the monster just in time. Once an insta-monster gets large enough to consume an entire building, it's usually impossible to return to its component parts." Alistair aimed his watch's monster-reversal function directly at the Gobblebox monster. "Okay," he said, "let's reverse this insta-monster! Let's separate the boy from the Gobblebox!"

"Don't forget to separate the Technobloks, too," I whispered.

A laser beam struck the Gobblebox monster on the forehead and its eyes flew open. The monster's Technoblok hair and fingers twitched.

Next, we heard a rumbling sound, and the Gobblebox's entire body shook.

And then:

KA-BOOM!

"Way to go, Alistair!" I held up my hand to give Alistair a high five. He looked confused for a moment, but then he slapped my hand.

Chauncey rubbed his head. "What happened? Where am I?"

"You passed out after eating too many marshmallows," I fibbed.

"Wait," said Chauncey, "wasn't I upstairs just a minute ago?"

"No," I lied. "You've been down here the whole time."

Chauncey frowned. "I don't feel so good."

"Maybe you better lie down on the couch for a minute before you walk home," said Alistair, helping Chauncey up from the floor.

"Uh, okay," said Chauncey. "But just for a minute."

Chauncey allowed Alistair to guide him to the couch as if he were a little old lady. "Nice watch," Chauncey mumbled, glancing at Alistair's wrist before he curled up and began snoring.

Alistair gestured toward the front room. "Psst!" Alistair whispered, pointing. "Iggy!"

Uh-oh, I thought, remembering that my little brother was still part insect. *What will Mom and Dad do when they see Iggy flying around the house?*

·30·

ELEVENTY-FORTY

IN THE FRONT ROOM, I found Iggy attempting to climb up the wall.

"Iggy!" Dottie yelled. "Come back down here!"

"Hey, Dano!" Iggy shouted, "Look at me!"

I noticed that Iggy's stinger was no longer visible, and his wings looked much smaller. *Interesting*, I thought. *Maybe the insect traits go away once he calms down.*

"Look!" Iggy tried to stand on the wall horizontally, with only two feet touching the wall. His insect grip must have been wearing off because he fell.

Luckily, I was there to break his fall just in time.

"No fair!" Iggy yelled. "I want STAND ON DAT WALL!"

"That's enough wall climbing," I said. "You must be tired after battling that monster."

"I NOT TIRED!"

"Fine," I said, "but just stop for a minute because I need to show you something in our room."

Iggy suddenly looked hopeful. "*Our* room?"

I realized it was probably the first time I had called it "our room" instead of "my room."

"Sure," I said. "The room is both of ours, right?"

"Okay, Dano!" Iggy zoomed past me and did a belly flop onto his bed.

"I have something for you, Iggy." I sat down on the bed and Iggy leaned his head against my shoulder. "Here, you can have this nice human norm- I mean, this nice pacifier."

"Mom say I not sposed to have dat."

"But this one is a special reward for attacking that monster."

Iggy stuck the pacifier in his mouth and closed his eyes. He looked happy.

"Thanks, Iggy," I said.

"Tanks why?"

"You helped rescue us from that Gobblebox monster. I guess you really were a superkid today."

"Like Squidboy," he said.

"Right," I said. "Like Squidboy."

"Dano," said Iggy, half asleep, "I glad you not eated pecuz I love you eleventy-forty, sixty-eight."

I knew that was Iggy's idea of the biggest number in the world.

I started to tell Iggy that eleventy-forty isn't even a real number, but then I changed my mind. "Me too, Iggy," I said. "I love you eleventy-forty, sixty-eight."

I guess I kind of like Iggy's quirks—his babyish words, his Squidboy underpants and Cinderella nightgown—even his freakish bug-DNA and everything. *Maybe sharing a room with Iggy won't be as terrible as I expected,* I thought.

And maybe having an alien for a friend isn't such a bad thing either.

· AFTERWORD ·

SO IN CASE you're wondering, Chauncey seemed normal enough after he took a nap on the couch. Luckily, he doesn't seem to remember that he turned into a cube-shaped monster and ate most of the objects in our kitchen, plus a couple of major appliances before Alistair changed him back into a regular boy. I think Alistair is just relieved that we got through this whole mess without losing his alien watch, and without anyone except me finding out that he's actually from Planet

Blaron. (I mean, Iggy kind of knows about the Blaronites, but nobody ever believes anything he says anyway, so that's okay.) For example, Mom and Dad didn't pay much attention when Iggy told them how he "flied around the house to sting dat monster!" And luckily, Iggy's wings and stinger completely disappeared after his nap with the Human Normalizer. Right now, Iggy looks just like a normal boy.

You'd never know from looking at him that he's secretly part insect—and that his secret identity is "Superkid-in-Training."